11/09 .

THE MADCAP

Other books by Nikki Poppen:

In this series:

Newport Summer

The Romany Heiress
The Heroic Baron
The Dowager's Wager

THE MADCAP

•

Nikki Poppen

AVALON BOOKS
NEW YORK

Published by Thomas Bouregy & Co., Inc.
160 Madison Avenue, New York, NY 10016

Library of Congress Cataloging-in-Publication Data

Poppen, Nikki, 1967–
    The madcap / Nikki Poppen.
        p. cm.
    ISBN (invalid) 978-0-8034-9987-4 (acid-free paper)
1. Heiresses—Fiction.   2. Americans—England—Fiction.
3. Nobility—Fiction.   I. Title.
    PS3616.O657M33 2009
    813'.6—dc22

                                                    2009025439

PRINTED IN THE UNITED STATES OF AMERICA
ON ACID-FREE PAPER
BY HADDON CRAFTSMEN, BLOOMSBURG, PENNSYLVANIA

Chapter One

San Francisco, Late Spring 1889

Marianne never saw it coming. It had been done with classic technique. The woman had waited until Marianne had acknowledged her. Then, when there could be no mistake about who was slighting whom, the woman had lifted her chin with a haughty air and sailed past without a flicker of recognition even though Marianne had shared the woman's box at the opera two nights prior. The worst thing in the world had happened for someone who aspired to be accepted by the social elite of New York. She'd been given the cut direct in the middle of a Patriarchs' ball and subsequently sent home in disgrace.

Amid the familiar comforts of her family's renowned San Francisco kitchen, Marianne Addison fought back the unpleasant memory and plunged her hands deep into

1

the thick ball of sourdough, pummeling the dough with all the force of her agitation. It had been three months since the *incident,* as she thought of it. She'd believed she'd put it behind her but a letter from her mother's friend in New York, full of news and gossip, had brought it all back. The letter had been innocuous enough, mentioning people she and her mother had met in New York before the incident. But it was enough to resurrect Marianne's anger. She'd been treated unfairly simply because she'd been different.

Marianne shoved the dough into a pan and set it on a shelf to rise. She grabbed another chunk of dough and set to work, starting the process all over again. She loved to make sourdough bread. She'd been doing it ever since she was a little girl and had tagged along with her father to the bakery. In those days, the bakery had been a small establishment on DuPont Street. Father would give her a chunk of dough and set her up at the big floury worktable while he went about his business.

With her hands busy in the dough, she could let her thoughts loose, spinning fairy tales full of castles and handsome princes. Today, her thoughts were far removed from fantasies. Today her thoughts were focused on the disaster of her visit to New York in January. Marianne punched the dough fiercely.

The adventure had started well enough. She and her mother had traveled in high style in her father's plush, private Pullman car, arriving at an elegant hotel with hot running water in her bathroom and other amenities she'd become used to in her father's large mansion on Powell Street back home. That was where the similarities between San Francisco and New York ended. In San Francisco, the only prerequisite for status was money. In New York, money wasn't enough, no matter how much you had. A girl also needed sponsorship from the right patron and acceptance by the right people.

Marianne had quickly learned the importance of that sponsorship among the Patriarchs, as certain men from Manhattan's ruling families were known. Without their patronage, there was little chance of an outsider being included in Mrs. Astor's prestigious Four Hundred Club, even temporarily.

Marianne sniffed and pushed back a strand of loose blond hair with a flour-covered hand. The whole premise was ludicrous. The only reason the Four Hundred Club was significant was because four hundred was the capacity Mrs. Astor could cram into her ballroom, Marianne thought uncharitably.

Of course, Marianne's mother had known all that beforehand and she had planned accordingly as best she could. Before the train had ever left San Francisco, they had been assured of invitations to the Academy of Music and afterward to the Opera Ball. There had been other guaranteed introductions as well. But the old saying that "blood will out" was never truer than in Manhattan. Better families than the Addisons had been cut by society simply for their questionable antecedents. She might be San Francisco's great

"Sourdough Heiress" today, but the Addison money was only two generations old and founded through her grandfather's sweat and hard work. There was nothing glamorous about the Addison family fortune, earned on the gold fields and in the streets of San Francisco when it had been Yerba Buena.

Manhattan had made it clear that her father, Cleveland Addison, could have been the richest man on earth and it wouldn't have changed the city's disapproval of him or of his daughter. Not even her mother's New England ancestry could prevail against the stonewall of Mrs. Astor's knickerbocker hierarchy. However, Marianne ruefully admitted with the wisdom of hindsight, it might have helped if she hadn't gone to that Champagne Sunday.

Marianne put the second loaf into a pan and checked the other one. She plopped down on a tall stool to wait, wiping her hands on her apron. The Champagne Sunday weighed on her mind.

Attending the dubious event had started out as a harmless dare between girlfriends. At least that was how it had appeared to Marianne at the time. Now she wondered if the other girls had known just how damaging the prank would be.

Sundays in Manhattan were notoriously boring. No social events were scheduled except for those that were held in a few suspect venues and hosted by women of ambiguous social character and attended by rich men looking for ways to escape the rigid pressures of their stifling Fifth Avenue mansions. It wasn't only men in attendance. Some women went too; Marianne had been assured of this by her so-called new friends. She soon found out these women were not the women with whom New York society socialized. These were the mistresses of the wealthy husbands, the opera singers and actresses who would never grace Mrs. Astor's ballroom. In short, they were Manhattan society's "unreceivables."

Too bad the evening had been so much fun. There had been singing and some dancing. Everyone had seemed much more relaxed than at the Patriarchs' balls. Marianne had enjoyed herself. But the aftermath had been horrendous.

She'd been given the cut direct two days later in the middle of a ballroom floor. Invitations had stopped immediately, a resounding endorsement of the cut. Her mother's pleading had found no sympathy. It had only taken their sponsor two days after the debacle to figure out that the situation was not redeemable by New York standards.

No one could be cut at a Patriarchs' ball and survive, especially not an arriviste whom Old New York didn't want in its midst anyway. Her mother had been quietly told that it would be best if they packed themselves back to San Francisco where society was more to their tastes. They would no doubt be bored in New York, they'd been told—the implication being that there would be no further invitations. They would spend the remainder of the social season in their elegant hotel suite with nowhere to go and no further expectations. When New York's best families removed to Newport in June, the Addisons would not be invited.

She had not deserved to be ostracized and she certainly hadn't deserved the disparaging comments the girls had made in quiet voices behind their fans. They'd meant her to hear, of course: "What can you expect? San Francisco society puts on airs but they're still so uncivilized, so showy and loud out there." The last had been said with derision, relegating San Francisco to the category of an oddity, a fraud only capable of superficially aping its betters.

The snub had hurt her as much as it had made her angry. Marianne loved her city with its hills and cable cars. She loved the sun bouncing off the bay, making the water sparkle. She loved the breeze that blew in from that bay, keeping the city cool. Most of all, she'd love a chance to show those girls in New York that she and San Francisco were better than all of them put together. But how to do it? What could she do that they couldn't copy?

She stood up and reached for a third loaf to knead. She massaged the dough, deep in thought. Her father would build a cottage in Newport if she asked, but that wasn't what she wanted. She didn't want to purchase her acceptance and the right to grovel at Mrs. Astor's feet. But Marianne recognized that attempting to break into their supercilious society wouldn't exactly be "besting" them, but becoming one of them.

She had to think. What did they covet that they couldn't readily obtain? Marianne smiled to herself. That was her father coming through in her thoughts. She'd once asked her father how he knew what to invest in. He'd said simply, "Find something people want and then find a way to give it to them. To do that, ask yourself, what do people want that they can't get for themselves?"

Marianne knew from years of watching her father do business that the best way to determine what people wanted was to look around and see what they admired in others. She thought of whom people at the social functions in New York had revered. Her mind lit instantly on the Earl of Camberly and his lovely wife, Audrey Maddox née St. Clair, once an American girl like herself and now the Countess of Camberly. They'd been the center of attention wherever they went, always in the presence of their friends the Carringtons. She'd had the good fortune to become acquainted with them. They may even have become friends if the incident hadn't interrupted her stay.

Now she had her answer. New York Society coveted a title. Not just any title, but an English title. This was something that couldn't be bought or constructed simply because one had enough money. Her idea formed quickly after that. New York would bow to her if she married an English lord. They would be sorry they had ever looked down their noses at her.

Her excitement grew. She set aside the dough and

wiped her hands on a towel. There were plans to be made, lists to be drawn up. This gambit would need meticulous strategies.

Marianne rubbed her hands together in delight, brushing flour motes into the air. After weeks of feeling directionless, she felt reborn. She had a purpose now. She was going to snare a lord. She was going to show them all! It never occurred to her as she sailed up the stairs to her room, humming under her breath, that she might actually succeed or that along with the title came a husband. Snaring a lord meant marriage when all was said and done. But if the thought crossed her mind, it did so fleetingly only to be pushed aside. There were so many steps to take before that marriage became a consideration that it was hardly worth dwelling upon.

She would have to plan this carefully. Fragments of a plan began to take shape. Throughout the afternoon, lists began to pile up at her writing desk as thoughts flew onto paper. By dinner that night, the plan had achieved full-blown maturity. Marianne was ready to launch the first phase of her stratagem: persuading her father to take the family to England.

Dinner was, without fail, an elegant affair at the Addison home at precisely seven o'clock every evening. Most nights, her father entertained business acquaintances or friends, many of them oftentimes unannounced until Cleveland Addison arrived with them in the drawing room. Such impetuosity would be frowned upon in New York with its social etiquette and calling-card rules. But in San Francisco the spontaneous gesture was welcomed as a matter of course.

Understanding her father's penchant for impromptu dinner parties, Elizabeth Addison and the well-run staff made sure the Addison dining room stood perpetually ready to accommodate guests with its long, polished table at which twenty people could easily be seated. The room and the adjacent drawing room were decorated impeccably and authentically in the style of Louis XV right down to the Sevres china that adorned the table, a tribute to the French chef who dominated Cleveland Addison's kitchen and made an invitation to dine at their table a most-coveted item among San Francisco's business community.

Tonight was no exception, Marianne thought, as she neared the drawing room at ten minutes before seven. Masculine voices drifted from the drawing room. She had hoped for the privacy of a family meal in which to launch her campaign, but guests might help her cause as well. Perhaps one of them could be unknowingly engaged as an ally.

Marianne smoothed the expensive silk of her jonquil evening gown and took a last look in the gilt-trimmed hall mirror to check that her coiffure was steady on her head. She gingerly touched the pile of neat curls gathered at the top of her head. A few random wisps had deliberately been left loose at her neck and Marianne reached for a strand of the pale blond hair and wrapped it around her finger, giving it a fanciful curl. She smiled, pleased with the results. She drew a deep breath and entered the drawing room, determined to see her plans launched with resounding success. After all, she was her father's daughter.

"Ah, there's my lovely daughter," her father's bluff tones announced from the fireplace where he stood talking with three of his guests. "Marianne, come and meet everyone." He waved her to his side. Marianne smiled as she made the acquaintances of the men dining with them. One of them had brought his wife and she was deep in conversation with Marianne's mother on the far side of the room. There wasn't time for much more than the usual exchange of small talk before the butler announced dinner. Once at the table, however, there was ample opportunity to broach the subject on Marianne's mind.

"Miss Addison, your father mentioned you are recently returned from New York," the guest on her right, a Mr. Green, said over lobster bisque.

"My mother and I were there in January," Marianne said politely. "We were there for most of the social highlights. We took in the opera on several occasions." No one at the table tonight, looking at her dressed her yellow silk and demure pearls, would ever suspect she'd been evicted from that rarefied society for her indiscretion in attending a Champagne Sunday.

The guests expressed sounds of interest at her trip.

"How did you find New York, Miss Addison?" the man across the table asked.

This was her moment—now, while she held everyone's attention. "I found it entertaining, although perhaps a bit confining with its Patriarchs and Mrs. Astor's Four Hundred. I did enjoy the museum, of course, and many of the cultural venues New York had to offer. I would like the opportunity to travel again."

"Travel back to New York?" Mrs. Green inquired.

Marianne sipped from her Waterford crystal wine glass. She was aware of her mother's eyes on her, wondering why she'd told such a lie. "A little farther than that, I think, next time. I'd like to try London. I've heard the National Gallery is not to be missed and the Season is a sight to behold." Marianne smiled at them all, saying disingenuously, "All those balls and Venetian breakfasts to attend sound positively wonderful. Just think of all the interesting people one would meet." She turned her gaze toward her father. "London in the late spring would be spectacular—quite the experience, don't you think, Father?"

Special experiences were one of her father's weaknesses. He was a man who staunchly believed life was a series of adventures. Certainly, most of his adventures were in the form of business risks, but he had compiled a lifetime of "experiences," from the imported French chef in his kitchen to the fleet of delivery wagons at the sourdough factory where he'd been one of the first people to expand their business by taking their product right to people's doorsteps.

"London, eh, Marianne?" Her father cocked an eyebrow at her. "What does your mother say to this?" He looked down the table to where Elizabeth Addison sat, still regal and lovely in her late forties, gracing the table with the kind of innate dignity one can acquire only through years of good breeding.

"London is a world away," Elizabeth said pointedly, shooting Marianne a questioning look. Marianne knew very well what her mother's veiled comment meant. London was more than geographically a world away; it was socially a world away too. London would take time to understand and would take practice. She knew her mother was skeptical. London would be no more welcoming of outsiders than New York had been. But there was one difference: in London, Americans, particularly rich Americans, were all the rage. Prince Albert adored American girls and the peerage adored their daddies' money.

"You must come too," Marianne said, turning back to her father. "The prince is obsessed with yacht racing. He's desperate to beat his nephew, Kaiser Wilhelm, at Cowes this year. The Earl of Camberly was talking about it in New York. He's crewed for the prince before."

The mention of yachting was a far more powerful lure for Cleveland Addison than was the prospect of hobnobbing with nobility. Still, Marianne noted that he looked suitably impressed at the mention of yachting and racing all in the same sentence. In addition to all else that he was, Marianne's father was a sporting man. In business or in leisure, he loved a good competition.

"I have been thinking of commissioning a new yacht. There's a boat builder out of Cherbourg who has an engine design I've been very intrigued with."

Marianne could see the wheels of her father's mind working as the soup was removed and the fish set down in front of him. "Well, Elizabeth, what do you say to a stop in France first?"

Marianne looked demurely down at her napkin, casting a covert glance in her mother's direction. "First? Before what?" she said obliquely.

"Why, before we head to London," he answered, full of bonhomie at the thought of his new yacht.

A frisson of excitement rippled through the table and the rest of the meal was taken up with discussion of London. The Greens had been there a few years past and were eager to offer suggestions.

Marianne beamed, barely able to contain her elation. She'd won round one. Her campaign to garner an English title was under way.

Chapter Two

London, May 1890

Alasdair Braden, the fourth Viscount Pennington, disguised a yawn with a sip of champagne from his glass. He stood on the perimeter of the dance floor with his friends, Gannon Maddox, the Earl of Camberly, and the American shipping magnate Lionel Carrington. All of them were doing their best to look cool, no mean feat considering the crush of people at the Bradley ball and the heat of the unusually warm spring evening. It did not help Alasdair's mood that he'd quarreled with his mother before he'd left her home in Richmond earlier that day.

Quarreling with one's mother was not an admirable trait in a gentleman but neither was being a man of five-and-thirty who let his mother run his life. *He* was the viscount, after all. He should be the one to decide. He knew very well what his duties and obligations were. How could he not, after having had them pounded into his head since he was eight? It wasn't that he didn't know his duty; it was only that he didn't care to do his duty with the woman his mother had picked out. He'd long harbored hopes that he would make a marriage that had less to do with duty and more to do with something more vivifying to one's personal well-being. But the time for such hopes was running out.

"You're in a sour mood tonight," Camberly commented, his eyes never leaving the dance floor where his bride of two years danced with an aging baron.

"I was merely wondering who the richest girl in the room was tonight," Alasdair said with ennui. "Then I realized it's the same every night. There's no difference." He waved a languid hand at the dancers swirling on the floor. "They're all the same. The richest girl in the room is still Pamela Hutchinson and she's still engaged to the Earl of Putnam's son. Nothing ever changes."

"Did you quarrel with your mother again?" Lionel nudged Alasdair with an elbow to the side, his face splitting into a teasing grin.

Lionel's good humor was instantly contagious and Alasdair found his spirits lifting a bit. It was no secret among the three of them that his mother was a consummate harpy. Alasdair chuckled. "She's determined to see me married by Christmas, and fancies a winter ceremony at the old pile," he said, referring to the Pennington seat in Devonshire.

"And who's to be the bride?" Lionel inquired in mock seriousness. They all knew—indeed it seemed most of London knew—who had garnered his mother's preference as the next Countess of Pennington.

"Sarah Stewart, as always. Mother and Sarah's father have been keen to join the estates for years and Sarah's father has a respectable amount of blunt, at least enough to keep the places going until the economy takes an upturn." Alasdair took another sip, unwilling to say anymore. Sarah was likable enough as a friend, even as a cherished friend. He'd known her since his childhood; fact was, he'd known her for her whole life. He'd been twelve when he'd gone to her christening. Therein lay the problem. There was something disturbing about having known one's bride when she'd been in her nappies.

Perhaps that was the whole problem with the entire Season, he groused. Everyone knew everyone and had for years. Alasdair knew, too, that he could no longer wait for the perfect bride. The situation with the estate had become dire. The luxury of remaining unattached had come to an end. He had to use the last asset he had and find a bride with extensive amounts of money this Season. Unfortunately, that last asset was himself and the august Pennington title.

The time had come for him to sell himself in matrimony. Of course, he had his pride. It wouldn't look quite that sordid on the surface. On the surface, it would appear that he was making yet another of the famous alliances the peerage were known for amongst themselves. But on the inside he would know what had finally dragged him to the altar and caused him to sacrifice his dreams of building something more with a wife.

His mother might truly be a harpy but it was not necessarily unwarranted. The family coffers were in danger of running dry. The agricultural depression had bled the estate, and although he hoped for an upturn, he had enough financial acumen to know the aristocracy would never be the same. Life as an idle, landed gentleman, living off the rents of others was a thing of the past. Relying on the land as a primary source of income to support over-large estates was a dangerous position to be in when one's social status rested on one's ability to lavishly and regularly entertain Bertie, Prince Albert. While Alasdair counted Bertie among his close friends, he scrimped and economized in order to accommodate a royal visit. He was very much hoping this year to avoid one altogether. He didn't want to need Sarah Stewart's modest fortune.

Sarah Stewart, his passably pretty neighbor, was the closest thing to an heiress he could find. Heiresses were in short supply in England, thanks to primogeniture and the male inheritance hierarchy. Alasdair knew that, for the sake of his family's security and position with the royal family, he might not have a choice. Sarah Stewart was fast becoming his only lifeline.

Regardless, he couldn't help but feel one more nail was being pounded into his proverbial coffin. He'd once naively believed that when he became the viscount, he'd be able to take back his life, make his own choices. But instead of freeing him, inheriting had only served to stifle his own desires even further. There was so little room for any expression of his own independence, his own wishes, in his life. At five-and-thirty, Alasdair Braden hardly knew who he was anymore beyond the physical embodiment of the Pennington title.

There was a flurry of commotion on the dance floor and a space opened up in the middle as people cleared out of the path of the oncoming dancers. Alasdair was riveted. The whirling pair was magnificent, waltzing in bold, sharp movements, their well-executed turns creating a large circle for them to move in undisturbed. They were dancing in the daring Viennese style, Alasdair soon realized. The woman was held far too close to the man's body for English standards, his arm not merely at the small of her back but wrapped around her waist to bring her near.

Alasdair recognized the man, Andrew Kentworth, the dashing heir to a respectable barony. Kentworth was young, but he should have known better. What could he have been thinking to induce a young lady to dance so perilously close to scandal? Then Alasdair looked at Kentworth's partner and knew precisely what the younger man was thinking. One look at the spun-gold hair of Kentworth's partner and Alasdair was quite certain Kentworth wasn't thinking at all.

In a room full of known commodities, Kentworth's partner was a newly lit candle burning brightly against the stark sameness of the other dancers. In a room filled with girls gowned in white satin and ridiculous frills, she shone in a gown of pale blue elegantly worked with a pattern of bronze swirls and curlicues. Instead of placing the focus on ruffles and bows, the dress relied on the wearer's form for its elegance. The gown's tailoring and high style bespoke Worth's stamp. The light from the chandeliers overhead glanced off the delicate seed-pearl trim of the gown's bodice and drew Alasdair's attention to the dancer's face.

She was enraptured by the dance and its breathless speed. He could see it in the smile on her face, the tilt of her chin as she looked slightly up at her partner, the cobalt glow in her shining eyes as she passed by Alasdair where he stood on the perimeter. He was dazzled by her. Intuitively, he knew he was struck by more than the image created by the expensive gown and the pearl-and-diamond collar about her slender neck, or by the rich pile of deep gold curls artfully pinned atop her head.

She was no still-life mannequin, another pattern card of English propriety. She was alive! Had he ever enjoyed a dance so thoroughly, found such pleasure in a piece of music? Been so completely true to himself in any given moment?

He had not realized he'd stepped forward until he felt Camberly's firm hand on his arm and his low whisper at his ear, "Easy, Dair."

"I must dance with her," Alasdair said simply. He stepped back from the floor but his eyes didn't leave the vision that had literally waltzed into his world. Never could he recall having been so intensely smitten.

He wasn't the only man who felt that way, Alasdair discovered twenty minutes later as he pushed his way through the throng that was gathered about her. But he might have a slight advantage: he had the Countess of Camberly to offer an introduction on his behalf. Alasdair had shamelessly cornered Camberly's wife the moment she'd returned from the dance floor. Audrey had the uncanny ability to know everyone at any given event and she did not fail him tonight. Not only did she know the young lady, but she'd had the good fortune to meet her when Camberly and Audrey had been in New York visiting her family last year.

"I never thought knowing an American would be so helpful," Alasdair murmured teasingly to Audrey who nudged through the crowd beside him.

"We have our uses." Audrey smiled, doing little to hide her amusement over his agitation. "There, we've made it." Audrey drew him forward with her into the inner circle standing around the lovely girl.

"Miss Addison, it's a pleasure to see you again."

Audrey offered the girl her hand to shake in the bold American custom. "Camberly and I enjoyed our visit to New York. I hope you did as well," Audrey said smoothly. Alasdair noticed how she'd discreetly slipped her name into the conversation to jog the girl's memory just in case. It certainly jogged the girl's mother's memory. Sitting beside the daughter was a woman of middle years bearing a strong resemblance to the beauty beside her. She sat up straighter, her eyes brightening at the mention of Camberly.

"Of course we remember you, Lady Camberly."

"My friend, Viscount Pennington, wished to make your acquaintance, Miss Addison." Audrey gestured in his direction and Alasdair hoped he wasn't smiling like a smitten fool. Miss Addison was far lovelier up close than she'd been on the dance floor. Her blue eyes sparkled when she turned her gaze his direction. Alasdair took her hand and bowed over it. "Miss Addison, it is a great pleasure to meet you. Might I prevail upon you for the next dance?"

Alasdair knew his request was most unorthodox. He was putting the young lady in the position of having to reject him outright if the slot was already taken, not a position in which a gentleman put a lady. After all, the whole point of dance cards was to avoid a scenario such as this. She tilted her pretty head and gave him a considering look. "I would love to dance, but I must decline since my dances are all spoken for." She held up her dance card. "A Lord Brantley has the next dance."

"Then I shall have to hope for better luck another time," Alasdair said politely. The girl needed to be more discerning, he thought privately. Simply putting a title in front of a man's name didn't make him respectable, and that was definitely the case with Brantley, who was as thorough a reprobate as any and barely received by decent families. The girl's mother should know better. English mothers did. But that was the difference between the English girls and the American ones. Alasdair had met American girls before. For all their forthright behaviors, they were incredibly naive when it came to navigating the intricacies of the British peerage.

Beside him, Audrey was saying something to the mother about coming to call, but Alasdair was eager to get away. He suddenly had a public service to render.

He used his height to scan the ballroom, looking for Brantley's blond head. Alasdair spotted him by a cluster of potted palms, deep in conversation with a group of men. He approached the group casually, catching snippets of the current conversation. Brantley and his group of inveterate gamblers were arguing the merits of the various horses racing at Ascot in a few weeks. A consummate gambler, Brantley was always on the prowl for the next big payoff to line his usually empty pockets. Those who knew his reputation best knew that the next big payoff wasn't only a gamble at the track or the tables but was often a gamble of a truly dangerous type, through more disreputable venues. It was oft whispered that he had engaged in some unsavory swindles a few years back on the Exchange and even in a few attempts at blackmail.

Alasdair grabbed a glass of champagne from a passing footman and easily insinuated himself into the conversation, offering opinions here and there on the different horses. He heard the music strike up for the next set of dances. Next to him, Brantley stirred.

"I've got to go and do my duty with the American chit." He gave a sigh, indicating he was less than pleased at having been corralled into the obligation. "She's a pretty little heathen, at least, and there's rumor her fortune is large enough to compensate for any other deficiencies."

Alasdair stiffened at the callous remarks, suddenly filled with chivalrous indignation. Brantley turned to leave the group and then something terrible happened. He bumped into Alasdair's right arm and Alasdair's nearly full glass of champagne spilled down the man's shirt front. Alasdair reached quickly for his handkerchief and offered it to Brantley, the very picture of a contrite apology.

"Oh, I'm *so* sorry. It was so incredibly clumsy of me." Alasdair said the words, all the while thinking the only thing clumsy about it was that he hadn't the foresight to take two glasses of champagne off the tray— one for his ploy to garner a dance and one for the cad's comments about Miss Addison.

"No harm, Pennington." Brantley dabbed at the large wet splotch. "Deuce take it, though. I can't very well go collect my partner with a wet shirt and smelling of alcohol."

"I'll be glad to stand in for you," Alasdair offered, stepping into the breach.

Brantley's eyes narrowed dangerously with speculation. "I am sure you would, Pennington. We all know that it's bad form to break an engagement with a lady. Give her my regrets, would you?" Brantley drawled in an ambiguous tone that only just hinted at hostility. Perhaps he had misjudged the man's supposed regret over dancing with Miss Addison. Perhaps Brantley's original attitude had been feigned. If so, Alasdair was more than glad to have thwarted the man's efforts to engage the unsuspecting Miss Addison.

"With pleasure," Alasdair said, slipping back into the crowd and wending his way back to Miss Addison's court. Within minutes, he explained how he'd carelessly spilled a full glass of champagne on her upcoming dance partner. Oh yes, he'd been most apologetic when he'd claimed Miss Addison for the dance, a lively polka, but he knew he wasn't sorry in the least.

"How kind you are, my lord, to come to my rescue," Miss Addison said while they took their places on the floor. "Is Lord Brantley a friend of yours?"

"No, we're not particularly close." Alasdair didn't bother to think about his answer. He was more interested in the intent blue gaze with which she fixed him, a whisper of a smile playing at her lips. Did she suspect?

The music started and the fast pace of the dance, while invigorating, left little opportunity for conversation. Alasdair didn't care. Miss Addison was light on her feet and threw herself into the energetic dance with all the vivacity she possessed. His spirits soared and for a few minutes, Alasdair felt free. All thoughts of Sarah Stewart and penniless estates eased from his mind and he lost himself in Miss Addison's joy.

The dance ended, leaving them breathless from their exertions, but she was still smiling, a coy, nuzzling smile that provoked his curiosity. "What is it?" he asked, cupping a hand beneath her elbow to guide her back to her mother.

"It all makes sense now."

"What does?" Alasdair replied, perplexed.

"Why you came to dance with me when Lord Brantley became indisposed," she said bluntly. "You've admitted not being friends with the man you replaced. It seems odd that someone who is not a friend would fill in for a mere acquaintance. I can only conclude that you spilled the champagne on him purposefully."

There it was in all its vaunted glory: American free speaking. By rights, he should have been offended. Such an accusation was hardly ladylike nor did the lady's bringing it up show him in an honorable light. But the only thing Alasdair could do was laugh.

"And if I did? Will you keep my secret, Miss Addison?"

"Will you come to call tomorrow?" she teased in return as those blue eyes of hers danced with mischief.

"Is this how blackmail is done in America?"

"*Blackmail* is such an ugly word," she bantered easily. "This is merely a reciprocal exchange of commodities between friends."

"Friend." Another reminder of her very-American nature. Such a term was used more conservatively in his circles. He was tempted to bring her attention to it. Friends after only a dance? Such a thing was not comme il faut in his circles. He elected to take a different tack. "A social call is the going rate for keeping a secret?" Alasdair affected a look of consideration. "I think I rather like this market."

It was time to give her back to her mother and the court of men awaiting her return. Alasdair reluctantly relinquished her, saying in low tones, "Until tomorrow." But he walked away with a spring in his step. At long last there was something to which to look forward.

Chapter Three

The hands of the long clock in the corner of the sitting room had hardly moved since the last time Marianne had discreetly checked them. Apparently, that had been less than a minute ago. Her mother coughed gently, indicating that Marianne hadn't been as discreet as she'd thought. She redoubled her efforts to pay attention to the guests seated around her. Several of the gentlemen she'd danced with the night before had called this afternoon with their sisters or mothers. But the only one she was interested in seeing again was conspicuously absent. Viscount Pennington had promised he'd call and Marianne was mentally holding him to it.

Dancing with him had been near magic. There was no question about his quality as a fine dancer but there was more to it. She'd danced with others who were accomplished in that regard as well. There'd been a certain polish about the viscount that set him apart from the others, a confident aura in the way he carried himself. Self-assurance had set well on his broad shoulders. He knew what he wanted and he'd wanted her. Not lasciviously by any means, unlike a few of the older men with whom she'd danced, who'd actually leered at her. Nor had he been assessing her value down to the last diamond and pearl in the necklace she'd worn as the controversial Lord Brantley had obviously done when he'd signed her dance card.

Truth be told, she was glad the viscount had ruined the man's shirt. She'd not been looking forward to dancing with Lord Brantley. The man was attractive in his way but his cold eyes had done nothing to veil his calculations. Marianne had known what he was about from the first.

Viscount Pennington, on the other hand, had given every sign that he wanted her for herself, that he simply wanted to be with her. She'd thought he'd enjoyed their dance immensely. It had been fun to match wits with him and she'd been impressed that he'd gone to so much trouble just to claim a dance when they both knew he could have merely waited for another night to dance with her. She had genuinely liked him and she'd thought he liked her. But he'd not come and she was more disappointed than she liked to admit.

Mr. Kentworth approached with his cousin Roberta

and his aunt, Lady Farnwick, to make their farewells, their fifteen minutes having come to an end. Marianne murmured something polite, barely hearing what they had to say. Others followed in his wake, making their gracious good-byes. In a little while, it would be too late. The clock that had moved so slowly throughout the afternoon now moved too quickly, ticking off the last ten minutes of their at home.

Her mother beamed as the drawing room of their rented town house on prestigious Portland Square emptied. "You've done well, Marianne. The gentlemen were so polite. Just look at all of the beautiful flowers they sent this morning. They were very thoughtful to bring their sisters and mothers today too."

They knew, without speaking of it, what that meant: invitations, which would allow them to claim another rung on the social ladder of acceptance. It wasn't the men who decided who was invited where, it was the women. Sisters and mothers and other female relations were important in navigating the shoals of Society.

Marianne gave a halfhearted smile. She'd truly thought that he would come. He'd seemed genuine and he was the only one she was interested in seeing again. It wasn't that he was the highest-ranking gentleman with whom she'd danced, nor was it his dark good looks. It was that he'd spilled champagne for her. A man willing to perform such contrivances for a chance to dance with her aroused all sorts of curiosity on her part.

Her mother reached over and patted her hand, divining Marianne's disappointment. "I'm sure we'll see him again, my dear. I'm quickly learning London isn't that big after all."

Just then the butler, a stuffy man named Snead, announced the arrival of one last guest. "The Viscount Pennington," he intoned.

Marianne smiled broadly and crossed the room to greet the new arrival in spite of her mother's hastily whispered words: "Don't appear too eager." Marianne held out her hand to shake, delighted that he was caught off guard only momentarily by the forwardness of her gesture. "I thought you'd changed your mind," she challenged lightly. "You left it until quite late."

The viscount had the good form to bow his head in deference to her scolding. "I am duly chastised, Miss Addison. However, in my defense, I wanted you all to myself." There was a twinkle in his coffee brown eyes when he met her gaze.

Immediately, Marianne saw his plan, how he'd arranged his arrival to attain his wish. By coming at the end of the at home, he'd ensured his being able to spend more than the requisite fifteen minutes with her. He was proving himself an ardent strategist. Marianne flashed a coy smile. "First the champagne and now this. How clever you are."

"How lovely you are," he replied neatly, presenting her with an enormous bouquet of flowers. He made a grand gesture toward the exquisite hothouse arrangements decorating various tabletops around the room. "I see I'm not the only one who thought to complement your natural beauty with nature's blooms."

Marianne took the bouquet from him, studying the flowers in delighted surprise. She noticed the difference right away. "But you're the only one who has brought a bouquet with purple of Romagna flowers." She inhaled deeply, enjoying the sweet fragrance. "They're grown in California. How did you get these?" Marianne was struck by the gesture. The flowers were thoughtful in the extreme and most likely had been exceedingly difficult to acquire.

"I have a friend who specializes in exotic blooms. He travels around the world on botanical expeditions. Fortunately, he'd acquired a few of these plants on a previous trip. I thought that with your being so far from home, you'd appreciate a small reminder of it."

A worrisome thought struck Marianne. "How did you know? I don't think I mentioned living in San Francisco last night." She was sure she hadn't. The polka had been too fast. They hadn't talked except on the way back to her mother and that conversation had been about his subterfuge to steal a dance.

The viscount gave her a charming, flirtatious smile. "I could mysteriously say I have my sources and leave you to wonder, but in actuality, I asked the Countess of Camberly."

Marianne hid her concern in another sniff of the bouquet. She wondered nervously what else the countess had imparted about her. Had the countess mentioned the debacle in New York? She hoped not. She reasoned that the woman wouldn't have bothered to introduce her friend to Marianne if the incident in New York mattered to her. Marianne hoped for the best. She shouldn't have been surprised that he'd sought out information about her. She was fast learning that was the way of the English ton. In San Francisco, people learned about each other through conversation with one another and were given a chance to prove themselves through their actions, but people in London Society didn't approach anyone without first being reassured of the other's status. One's reputation was often previously established before an introduction even took place. No one risked meeting someone who might prove to be entirely unsuitable.

Marianne took a final smell of the flowers and gathered her wits. "I must get the flowers in water right away. Will you excuse me? You can sit and become better acquainted with my mother." Marianne moved to go in search of a vase when the viscount raised his eyebrows slightly in the direction of a footman, who stepped forward instantly and offered his services. "Miss, I'll see to those for you."

Marianne blushed and relinquished the bouquet. "I forget how it is here. Sometimes it seems so silly to have someone do such a little thing one is capable of doing themselves." Silently, she chided herself. What a stupid thing to forget! He probably had a house full of servants. Now he'd think she was an uncultured American. They had a staff of servants at home too, but it didn't preclude doing things for oneself.

"Come sit down, Lord Pennington." Her mother gestured to the chairs gathered around the settee to cover the awkward moment. "Will you take tea?"

"I'd be delighted." He took a chair near the settee, crossing his long legs with casual ease. "I confess that I had ulterior motives for arriving so late in the afternoon, Mrs. Addison. I was hoping Miss Addison would do me the pleasure of accompanying me on a drive through the park."

"I'd love to." Marianne didn't wait for her mother to answer for her although the question had been directly asked of her.

Half an hour later, Marianne sat in the handsome viscount's curricle, with a straw hat trimmed with cream veiling that matched her pale pink and cream driving ensemble, perched atop her head, her maid riding on the back platform as a discreet chaperone.

The viscount expertly tooled the curricle through the Mayfair traffic to Hyde Park. Marianne didn't mind the slow pace. It gave her time to study the man who'd spilled champagne on another as the price for a dance. She'd half feared her memories of him from the prior night were somewhat magnified but he was indeed as handsome as she remembered, perhaps even more so. His nut-dark hair shone in the dappled sunlight filtering through the park's leafy trees. In profile, his nose stood in sharp relief against the planes of his face. His jaw carried a certain strength to it, reminding her this was the face of a man, not a fresh-shaven boy who had yet to come into his prime. In comparison to the other young men who'd called, the difference was remarkable.

Everything he did bespoke an impressive aura of confidence. He greeted people who passed them in similar vehicles while he smartly steered his curricle through tight spots on the path crowded with walkers, riders and other drivers. It seemed he knew everyone. They could hardly move twenty feet without encountering another of his many acquaintances. At each encounter, he endeavored to introduce her as "Miss Addison of San Francisco."

It was quite overwhelming to be the center of so much attention. The effect was not lost on her. She knew enough to understand that association was of the utmost importance in London. After today, the two of them would be linked together in conversation. People would say at tea tomorrow or at supper parties tonight, "I saw Pennington in the park today. He was driving with the Addison girl from San Francisco." The comment would inevitably be followed with another commentary on whether or not such an activity passed censure.

"Do you know everyone?" Marianne asked after yet another greeting.

He turned toward her with a laugh. "I do. Don't you?" he joked.

Marianne shook her head. "I marvel at how anyone can keep it all straight. The forms of address alone are overwhelming. I can't begin to fathom the intricacies of dinner seating."

He gave her a questioning look. "Don't you seat people by rank in America?"

Marianne wished she hadn't brought it up. He was staring at her with an incredulous look. "We do, but it's much simpler. Seating is all about money. Whoever has the most sits at the top of the table and we work our way down from there."

She thought the viscount might be repulsed by the gaucheness of the notion. But he merely laughed again and said, "How very democratic." He pulled the curricle onto the verge, away from the flow of traffic. "Would you like to walk a little? There's a duck pond not far from here—and we're not likely to be interrupted by all the people I know," he added with a grin, stepping to her side of the carriage and swinging her down with ease.

"Now we have enough quiet for a real conversation," he said as he led her down to the pond and an empty bench nearby. "Tell me about San Francisco, your home, Miss Addison. All I know is what I've read about it in Kipling's article on it not long ago. It seems like a most interesting town."

It was all the encouragement Marianne needed to

regale him with tales of her home, from the enormous twenty-five-room mansion on Powell Street to the first bread factory her father owned on DuPont Street.

"You sound as if you miss it," the viscount said sympathetically when she broke off her stories.

Marianne nodded. "I do. We've been gone for several months. There was the time spent traveling across the United States, of course, and then we spent a few months in Paris and went on to Italy briefly before we came to London." All in an attempt to gain some Continental polish and practice. There'd been her clothes to order from Worth, lessons in British comportment, and her father's new yacht to check on in Cherbourg. One could not assail the bastion of London society without practice and the right tools. Even then, Marianne had discovered that she wasn't willing to remake herself entirely simply to fit in.

She had the right tools: the Worth wardrobe, the prestigious address on Portland Place, the invitations into the desirable social sets. None of that could change her, though, and she found that she didn't want to be changed. For instance, she liked getting a vase in which to put her flowers. She doubted she'd ever get used to someone doing those simple tasks for her.

The viscount began to ask another question. "Miss Addison—"

Marianne shook her head. "Please, call me Marianne. Everyone at home does." She didn't care how unorthodox or bold the request was.

"Then you must call me Alasdair, or Dair as my close friends do." He smiled, his coffee-colored eyes sparkling their approval. Marianne thought she could stare at those warm, dark depths all day without boring of it.

"Now, it's your turn to tell me about you," Marianne said, turning the conversation. "What do you do when you're not in London?"

A shadow flickered across Alasdair's face at the question, and his eyes seemed to go flat and cold momentarily.

"I didn't mean to pry. My apologies," Marianne offered quickly. She looked away, giving her attention to the activity on the pond. A little boy stood at the water's edge sailing a small toy boat on a string.

"No, it's just that I've spent a large part of my time recently trying to figure out the answer to your question. Who am I?" He broke off. "I'm sorry, that's not what you expected to hear. I haven't made it easy for you to make conversation. I am at fault."

Marianne opened her mouth to reply, but just then the little boy let out a loud cry of disappointment. His boat had come loose from its string and capsized in the pond not far from where they sat. He let out a wail.

Marianne looked around. The boat wasn't more than eight or nine steps from shore, too far for a little boy to wade out but surely not too far for an adult. The boy's nanny was alternately consoling him and scolding him for setting up such a racket. But beyond that, no one sitting on the benches or strolling nearby did anything. Marianne's heart went out to the boy who'd lost the boat. If no one was going to come to his aid, then she would.

"Oh dear," Marianne said, reaching to undo her shoes. "I suppose my stockings are done for."

"Marianne, whatever are you doing?" Alasdair queried in a confused whisper.

"I'm going in after the boat. I don't think the pond is all that deep at this point." She gathered up her pale pink skirts and made her way down to the shoreline before Alasdair could dissuade her. She called a few words of reassurance to the little boy who managed to stop crying in order to watch her. She heard Alasdair's footsteps behind her. She supposed she'd shocked him.

Again.

She was apparently in the habit of doing that. But going after the boat was the only real solution available. It took her only a few moments to retrieve the boat. Alasdair was there at the water's edge to help her back up the bank to the bench, his hand warm and supportive on her arm.

Marianne thought she'd performed the task more than admirably. She'd managed to ruin just her stockings. The pond had turned out to be quite shallow, as she'd suspected, and her skirts were only the tiniest bit damp. The look on the boy's face when she returned the boat was recompense enough for the ruined stockings.

She even managed the silliness of retreating behind a tree to modestly remove the ruined hosiery before putting her shoes back on. It was beyond her why she couldn't simply sit on the more-comfortable bench and take off her stockings, or why she couldn't have gone into the pond barefoot to start with.

But by then the damage was done. It was too late to avoid being the target of gossip. Obviously, English-women didn't make a habit of wading in Hyde Park or rescuing toy boats. A hard stare from Alasdair in the direction of the onlookers, however, sent them shuffling on their way.

Her stockings successfully removed, Marianne plopped back down on the bench next to Alasdair, who stared at her with an indecipherable look on his face. She worked the fastenings of her shoes, suddenly self-conscious of his attentions. Perhaps this was where he politely offered to drive her home and then disappeared from her life. Perhaps he was already regretting having introduced her to so many people.

"What is it? You're staring," Marianne said at last, unable to bear his scrutiny.

"My apologies."

She looked up and saw the hint of a smile on his lips. "Marianne, are you attending the Stamford ball to-night? If so, would you save me a waltz?"

Marianne cocked her head to the side, intent on not giving in too easily, although relief coursed through her in heady amounts. He wasn't going to reject her out of hand. "I think that could be arranged without too much effort."

Alasdair rose and offered her his arm. "Shall we drive on, then? We've done our good deed for the day."

He was laughing with her, flirting with her again, and Marianne gladly returned his banter. On the way back to her home, they talked of her impressions of London, Alasdair taking care to point out places of interest during the drive. Marianne had the easy feeling that she'd known Alasdair for far longer than a day and it felt positively marvelous.

"I've a confession to make," Marianne said as they drew to the curb in front of her home.

"Oh, a confession?" Alasdair raised his eyebrows in shocked good humor. "More scandalous than rescuing boats from duck ponds?" he teased.

Marianne pretended to consider it for a moment. "Well, somewhere between duck ponds and spilling champagne for a dance," she answered back. "The truth is, I'm glad you spilled champagne all over that Lord Brantley. I didn't like him. Something didn't seem right about him. I'd much rather dance with you anytime."

Alasdair nodded. "It's not for me to malign a fellow peer without cause. However, you would do best to stay away from Lord Brantley. He has certain habits I am sure you would find distasteful, to say the least."

Marianne laughed. "The English are unfailingly polite even when describing a bad seed."

Alasdair came around to help her down. "I assure

you, Marianne, that we too have tempers when provoked."

He walked her to the door and gallantly bent over her hand. "Until tonight, Miss Addison." He was suddenly all English formality again.

Marianne couldn't resist one last tease before he left. "Is this how you say you don't disapprove of my having fished a boat out of the drink?"

He looked at her, mastering a level of solemnity with his gaze while his mouth twitched with a wry half grin. "Yes, Marianne, I believe it is."

London was infinitely more exciting with Marianne Addison at his side, Alasdair reflected a week later. He made it a point to dance with her every night and to send her hand-picked flowers every day, including purple of Romagna when he could cajole it out of his botanist friend. He'd come up with an endless amount of excuses to be wherever she was in the afternoons; not drives in the park, not Venetian breakfasts, not even shopping trips were beyond the pale of his efforts.

He was not alone in his attention or attraction to Marianne. Marianne Addison, openly known now among the ton as the Sourdough Heiress, was fast becoming London's latest cause célèbre. There were some who labeled her an Original for her loveliness and exuberance, and others who labeled her merely the latest American novelty.

The latter group expected her to eventually overstep

the boundaries of acceptable behavior and be sent packing home as other American girls had been in the past. Many expected that such an eventuality wasn't too far in the offing. The very items that made Marianne an Original were the same items that made her controversial.

Whether she knew it or not, whether she cared or not, she walked a fine line between the freshness of her actions and the unacceptable nature of them. There were those who disapproved of her clear enjoyment of dancing. In addition, word of the duck pond incident had circulated around drawing rooms for a few days until it had been squelched by a well-placed remark from the Countess of Camberly, who'd said it proved hard to gossip negatively about someone doing a good deed.

After that, those who were convinced Marianne Addison would not "take" in London didn't dare voice such sentiments out loud in certain company for fear of reprisal. The prince liked high-flying American girls and Alasdair was the prince's friend. Instead, the would-be naysayers would have to wait and let Marianne orchestrate her own fall, after which the handsome, eligible Viscount Pennington would surely turn his attention back to proper English girls.

Alasdair was aware of these undercurrents even if Marianne wasn't. Still, she was guilty of nothing more than vivacious dancing, saving a small boy's boat, and having stolen the attentions of an eligible peer. Ironically, it was the last of these faults that caused Alasdair the most trouble. Before June had reached its midpoint, rumors of his attachment to the fascinating American parvenu brought his mother to town.

Chapter Four

Alasdair rounded the corner to his Bruton Street
town house, whistling a lively tune that was indicative
of his exceedingly good mood. He'd squired Marianne
and her mother on a trip to Hatchards booksellers in
Piccadilly that morning. Marianne had been amazed
at the selection of books, doing nothing to disguise her
unabashed excitement at exploring the establishment
and commenting on its treasures. No English girl, especially not Sarah Stewart, who Alasdair doubted had
read a whole book from cover to cover, would have
displayed such satisfaction. Alasdair couldn't recall a
time he'd had a conversation with a woman about a
book; yet he and Marianne had discussed not one
book, but several, while they browsed the shelves.

The tune and his good humor faded abruptly when

he saw the black carriage parked outside his home. There was nothing like an unannounced visit from his mother to quash his high spirits.

Alasdair squared his shoulders and mounted the steps. "How long as she been here?" he quietly asked a footman in the foyer.

"A little over an hour, milord. She's taking tea in the Yellow Salon," the footman informed him.

"Very good," Alasdair said. He tugged at his waistcoat and strode down the hall to the Yellow Salon, one of the private rooms strictly for family use when they were in residence, which thankfully wasn't often. Most of his extended family preferred their country homes to life in Town. Even his mother preferred to stay in Richmond during the Season.

The Yellow Salon was a small, cozy chamber done in sunny shades of yellow and white striped wallpaper. The space was furnished with a sofa in jonquil brocade and a pair of matching winged chairs. Around the room, vases of blue violet gladioli decorated tabletops, adding a brilliant splash of color—just the shade of Marianne's eyes. The odd thought crossed his mind that Marianne would look stunning in this room.

But Marianne wasn't the woman sitting at the settee in the room's center. His mother, Margaret Braden, the dowager Viscountess Pennington, set down her teacup and fixed him with her stare. "There you are at last."

Alasdair's jaw tightened. She made it sound as if he were an errant child, overdue from his adventures, when in fact, she was the unexpected guest. He tamped down on his desire to return the petty scold. "Mother, this is an unexpected pleasure. What brings you to Town? I didn't think you were coming up until after the Derby." Alasdair settled himself casually in a winged chair facing the sofa. He reached for a lemon scone. If he had to deal with his mother, he might as well enjoy Cook's excellent baking.

"Pleasure has nothing to do with it," she snapped. "What has brought me to Town is you. It has come to my attention that you've comported yourself poorly by attaching yourself to a wild American girl. It's dreadfully insensitive of you when there are so many English girls available who would love to marry you. And really, Alasdair, there's no need to do anything at all beyond the basic courtesies of fulfilling your social obligations. You have Sarah waiting for you at home. In fact, I could invite her up to stay in Town."

"Town would make her uncomfortable," Alasdair ground out in Sarah's defense. He valued Sarah's friendship; he just didn't want to marry her if he could avoid it. Sarah was a country girl at heart, preferring the meadows and villages of Devonshire to the noise and havoc of London. Sarah would hate London, and London would intimidate her.

"Well, you've certainly made *me* uncomfortable with all of these rumors about the American girl. I am sure you can't imagine how I felt hearing this lurid gossip about you in the middle of a tea. I'd just taken a bite of scone when Lady Harmon said, 'I hear Pennington has taken up the latest fad of falling for a rich American.' I looked her squarely in the eye and denied it. I said, 'I know of no such thing. He has an understanding with Miss Sarah Stewart.' "

His mother leaned forward, gathering a full head of steam. "Then Lady Harmon stared at me with that falsely innocent gaze of hers and said, 'Then I suppose it's not true that the American has danced the waltz in scandalously close proximity to your son every night since they met, or that he took her driving in Hyde Park where she waded in a duck pond with her stockings on?' "

"She's not wild, Mother," Alasdair broke in. "She waded in to retrieve a toy boat, and there's nothing wrong with the Viennese waltz except that it's not called the English waltz."

His mother sucked in her breath, horrified. "Then you don't deny it?"

"There's hardly anything worth denying, Mother." Alasdair leaned back in his chair, a leg crossed over his knee.

When it became obvious he wasn't going to quarrel with her, Alasdair's mother sighed and changed her tack. "I understand everyone's doing it, these days: Marlborough and the Vanderbilt chit, Camberly and his American wife. Bertie's penchant for the American girls doesn't help. His own proclivity spurs the others on. The Carlton Club Set, the Marlborough Set, all have made a novelty out of American girls. I dare say it's only their fortunes that make the girls so attractive to our men. If they didn't have their money, I doubt anyone of merit would take them seriously," she opined.

Alasdair thought of Marianne's joie de vivre and privately disagreed. In fact, he hadn't thought once about Marianne's financial background. Of course he knew, as did all of London, that she was heir to a staggeringly large fortune built on bread baking. She and her parents made no attempt to hide the fact. She wore a Worth gown every night, fully turned out with the proper accessories. The pearl-and-diamond choker she'd worn the first night was worth a small fortune alone. But such mundane matters had been quickly obscured by her natural vivacity.

His mother studied him. "Perhaps I have misunderstood the situation. Is it the money? Is she quite rich?" His mother became somberly melodramatic. "Oh, my son, I see now that you're doing this for the family—sacrificing yourself to the American dollar, all for the sake of our financial well-being."

It was obvious that she honestly believed it to be the case; her speech was so sincere. One would think her son was sacrificing himself on the altar of his country for some patriotic deed. If circumstances had been different, Alasdair would have laughed out loud. But she was serious and that was no laughing matter. He didn't want his mother countermanding any rumors with her version of the truth.

"No, Mother, that is not why I have been linked to Miss Addison," Alasdair said flatly. "I rather like her and we get along splendidly. I've found we have many things in common."

She heaved a sigh, feigning resignation. But Alasdair was experienced enough with her shenanigans to know she was nowhere near as resigned to the situation as she pretended to be. "I suppose a man is entitled to one last fling, one last brush with scandal, before he settles down."

Alasdair rose, effectively putting an end to the conversation, it was going nowhere anyway. "This is not a 'fling.' Not even Bertie trifles with unwed girls, American or otherwise. Regardless of my relationship with Miss Addison, I have no intentions of marrying Sarah Stewart. I have made this clear to you in the past and I am making it clear once again."

A hand flew to her throat. "You can't mean to marry the American girl! Sarah has enough money and she's English."

"I don't know what I intend, Mother, however I do know that I will not marry at anyone's whim but my own." The frustrating part about arguing with his mother was that he held his ground, spoke his mind without reservation, and it didn't matter—she simply ignored his decisions.

She was about to launch another round of argument.

Alasdair raised his hand to forestall it. "Excuse me, Mother. I have appointments to keep this afternoon."

Alasdair's so-called appointments were nothing more than a meeting with Lionel and Gannon at White's. He was early, but arriving ahead of schedule was preferable to listening to his mother's arguments. He sank into a deep chair, prepared to enjoy a freshly pressed edition of the *Times*. He hadn't gotten far into the financial news when Lord Brantley approached, flanked by two of his gambling cronies.

"I am starting to think it was no accident you spilled champagne on my shirt," Brantley began without preamble, taking a chair uninvited. "I was rather suspect that night, and seeing how things have turned out, I'm quite convinced I was right. You spilled on purpose."

"Accidents are accidents, Brantley, *because* they don't have causes or explanations," Alasdair remarked, not setting aside his paper and thus hoping to make the message clear that he wanted to be left alone. "I do hope the stain came out, at any rate."

Brantley didn't take the hint. He settled into the chair comfortably, giving the impression of committing himself to a lengthy conversation. Alasdair had never spoken with Brantley for more than a span of minutes. He couldn't guess what the man had to discuss with him now.

"Oh, the stain came out as did the news that *my* intended partner for that dance is a bonafide heiress to a multimillion-dollar fortune. Did you know that night? I think you did," Brantley said coldly. "I should have been the one dancing with her. But instead it was you, and now you've been seen everywhere with her. Both the *World* and the *Morning Post* have noticed you've made a regular habit of dancing with her." Brantley tossed a newspaper at him, the paper folded back to the appropriate page.

Alasdair took a moment to scan the article. It was the usual social news, one-line mentions of who had been seen where and with whom. He scanned a few lines before one section leapt out at him: "A certain Viscount P___ has been seen in the company of the newest American heiress to visit London. The said American, Miss A___, is the daughter of a sourdough bread baker from San Francisco. Her father is reported to be worth millions. This author wonders if her main attraction for Viscount P___ is her bank account. While it is not known for certain, it would not be beyond the realm of possibility that Viscount P___ is looking for a way to bolster flagging family coffers before the situation becomes dire."

Alasdair fought his rising temper. It would serve no purpose for Brantley to sense his frustration. Showing his anger would only be seen as a validation that the rumors about his finances were true, something he'd worked hard to keep away from prying gossips.

"What's your point, Brantley? The social columns are full of half-truths. The writer even admits it is all speculation." Alasdair gave a cynical chuckle. "Surely you don't believe everything you read?"

Brantley leaned forward, his voice low and menacing. "The point is that she should have been dancing with me. You stole my chance. Like any other rich American, she's probably hanging out for a title. Mine would do just as well as yours in that case. She probably doesn't even know the difference between a baron and a viscount. You wanted her for yourself and you deliberately undermined my attempts."

"As I recall, you didn't seem overly disappointed," Alasdair shot back, his temper rising now at the disparaging remark about Marianne.

"I have my pride," Brantley said coldly. "What else was I to do that night?"

"I see." Alasdair did see. Brantley had feigned ennui over the prospect of dancing with the American to save face, as he'd suspected. Of course the man couldn't look desperate in front of his friends.

But hearing the man slander Marianne and talk so crassly about her motives caused Alasdair's protective hackles to rise. He was doubly glad he'd spilled the champagne on Brantley. He only wished it had been more. The blasted man saw Marianne as a financial remedy. He saw none of the qualities Alasdair had come to appreciate about her: her quick wit, her sharp insights, the joy she took in each day.

It was something of an irony that finances were now the reason he, himself, was being cited for an interest in Marianne, a reason that had never initially crossed his mind.

Brantley rose and brushed at his trousers. "Well, I doubt she'll last long. Already, her behavior is catching up to her. She's too wild by half. It's quite shocking really, all that hand shaking and that stunt at the duck pond. Some people can't be brought up to snuff no matter the size of their wardrobe and of their daddy's bank account," Brantley said derisively. The two men with him laughed in agreement. "In fact, I'd wager she'll be gone before the Season ends. Miss Addison won't last until August before London casts her aside. Anyone willing to take the wager? Pennington, you've been her champion thus far," Brantley suggested.

Alasdair looked coldly at Brantley and shook his newspaper open. He would not be a party to such a bet nor would he rise to Brantley's rather obvious bait. He turned his attentions to an article on American wheat. But the damage was in no way mitigated by his absence from the conversation.

"I'll take your bet. Sounds rather interesting," said one of the men with Brantley, Lord Hamsford, a dissipated individual whom Alasdair knew only by name. "You say she'll be ousted by the end of July, by the Cowes Regatta. I'll say August fifth for good measure. Perhaps we can even help the cause along."

The men strolled over to the famed betting book and entered their contract. Alasdair was disgusted. More than disgusted, he was genuinely worried for Marianne.

The last comment Hamsford made was truly alarming. The depths to which Brantley would sink in order to win a bet knew no bounds. There was no doubting that her naïveté and her outgoing nature would continue to land her at the center of London's attention for better or for worse. Alasdair did not want to see that used against her in a destructive manner. He had not wanted to be part of Brantley's crass wager but his concern for Marianne drew him in, regardless.

There was only one way she'd escape Brantley's petty revenge and that was if someone brought her up to standard. Alasdair would do what he could. But ultimately, Marianne would need more than him. Alasdair put aside the newspaper and glanced at his pocket watch. Camberly would not have left his house yet. There was still time to catch him. Hastily, Alasdair scribbled a note for Lionel telling him to meet them at Camberly's town house. If there was anyone who knew how to be an acceptable American among the English it was Camberly's wife, Audrey St. Clair.

"Brantley is a scoundrel," Lionel remarked an hour later in Camberly's music room where the three were assembled with Audrey. Lionel made no attempt to hide his displeasure over the latest development. "He must realize that the wager alone is enough to cause a scandal. No decent woman is named in White's betting book."

"He understands perfectly well what he's done."

Alasdair paced the length of the room, hands shoved deep into his trouser pockets. "What's worse is that his friends are determined to play along. One of them even suggested trying to 'help things along.'"

Audrey's temper flared. "They mean to compromise her on purpose simply to win a bet?"

Alasdair turned to Audrey. "I'm not sure they intend to go that far but they do intend to see her set up for failure."

"That hardly seems fair."

"Men like Brantley don't have to consider fairness, Aud." Camberly spoke from his chair. He'd been relatively silent, content to let the others vent their frustration. "His reputation as an honorable man was shredded long ago. He cares for nothing beyond money and his own self-importance." The room fell silent.

"I'm not sure we can protect her, Dair," Lionel said at last.

"There must be a way. She doesn't deserve to be the butt of Brantley's scheme. She's quite the unwilling pawn in all of this. None of it's her fault. She's merely been singled out because she's different and because of me."

"It's happened before," Audrey said quietly from the settee.

"What's happened before?" Alasdair stopped pacing in front of the fire place mantel.

"Marianne has been singled out before, in New York, the winter we were there. It wasn't pleasant but she survived. She's here, after all. Then, too, it wasn't her fault." Audrey tapped her chin with her finger. "Lionel is right—we can't protect her. But we can make sure she succeeds. It will be the campaign of the Season. We'll start tonight."

Chapter Five

The Radcliffe Musicale had the unique distinction of being a musical evening that actually produced quality musical talent compared to several other such evenings that showcased the mediocre talents of this year's crop of debutantes. Over the years, it had become the unstated norm that only the best musicians among them would volunteer their talents for the Radcliffe Musicale. Those with lesser skills were expected to hold themselves in check that evening and become part of the audience.

To reinforce the high standards of the night, the Radcliffe home on Curzon Street was turned out in all its glory. The chandelier in the main foyer cast brilliant light up the grand staircase to the ballroom that had been partitioned into a slightly smaller venue for the evening. Inside the ballroom, potted plants and gilt screens had been set up to minimize the enormity of the room, as the event had outgrown the music room in which it had been originally hosted. Chairs were set up in neat rows around a temporary stage that had been erected for the evening. The piano had been moved from the music room to the impromptu dais and other instruments were propped up along the edge.

It was very impressive to behold, Marianne thought, as she walked through the door with her parents, her father having just arrived back from a quick trip to Cherbourg. They had been invited to the event by Camberly himself, but since the earl's wife was playing the piano that evening and had to be present earlier, the Addisons arrived on their own.

Marianne and her mother greeted a few of the people to whom they'd been introduced over the past weeks but the larger span of Marianne's attention was spent searching the room with her eyes for a sign of Alasdair. She had not encountered him yet today at any of the places she'd gone. It was the first time in several days she had not seen or heard from him in some way, and the day seemed incomplete, unbalanced in some indistinguishable way without him.

She was aware of how odd such a realization was. She'd only known Alasdair for a few weeks. Yet in that time she'd become accustomed to his presence. If she'd been asked who she'd acquired as a friend during her time in London, she would have said him.

Mrs. Farnwick and her daughter, Roberta, stopped to say hello. Roberta smiled knowingly, catching Marianne's distraction. She linked her arm through Marianne's and drew her aside. "The viscount will be here, don't worry. He'll want to hear the countess play the piano."

Marianne cast her eyes downward. She'd best be careful not to give herself away so completely. It wasn't proper for a girl to seek out the attentions of a gentleman even if he was just a friend. In America, it had been far more common for young men and women to mix socially than it was here. She'd gone on any number of picnics with other young people of her social station in San Francisco. But here, Marianne had been surprised to learn just how cloistered girls were until they came of age.

"Would you care to stroll with me around the room, Miss Addison?" Roberta asked. "We can walk past the refreshment table. I've heard the Radcliffes have a carved-ice swan for the centerpiece that's supposed to be magnificent."

Several other young women strolled the perimeter of the room with their friends, heads close together as they chatted. It was the perfect ruse for sharing gossip and showing off one's lovely gown all at the same time. Marianne sensed that Roberta Farnwick was disposed to use the activity for the same reason, although she couldn't imagine what Roberta would want to gossip about with her. After all, Roberta was not a close acquaintance.

They passed the long tables of refreshments set against the far wall out of the way of the performance area and made the obligatory comments about the ice swan. A length of silence fell as their conversation diminished. Marianne had no idea how she'd fill the time until their walk was completed. She didn't know Roberta all that well and she'd exhausted her store of small talk. She needn't have worried.

Roberta had things to say. "Miss Addison, you are new to London, and as such is the case, I feel I must inform you of some bad news," Roberta said, her voice so quiet that Marianne had to lean quite close to pick up the other girl's words. "The viscount is not exactly an eligible *parti*, my dear." Roberta fussed with the fan hanging from her left wrist. "This is so difficult to say, but you must know. He's all but betrothed to a Miss Sarah Stewart, who prefers to stay in the country. It's not official but everyone knows his mother and her father have been promoting this match for eons. Their estates share a border."

A cold pit formed in Marianne's stomach. Alasdair was to marry another? Everyone knew? It did come as something of a shock. Surely he would have mentioned it. Then again, mentioning it may not have crossed his mind. If everyone knew, he probably felt there was no reason to bring it up. It could be easy to forget that newcomers wouldn't know something that had become de rigueur for everyone else.

And why bring it up when it wasn't relevant to their friendship? If she was disappointed by the news, it was her fault. He'd not spoken outright of any desire to court her, nor had he spoken any inappropriate words of love. There were no expectations except the ones she'd created in her head, and even those certainly had not gone as far as marriage. She simply enjoyed being with him. She'd come to count on his friendship—that was all. Roberta Farnwick simply misunderstood the situation.

"I am happy for him, then," Marianne replied. "I didn't know, of course, being so new to Town. The viscount has been a good friend to me during our brief acquaintance. I would wish nothing but the best for him." She wanted to be clear with Roberta as to exactly what the status of her relationship to Pennington was. Perhaps she also wanted to be clear with herself, just so her heart and mind didn't misunderstand one another.

Roberta stifled a laugh. "Friend? My dear, since when have men and women been friends? It's simply not done. What's the point anyway? After one marries, one has to give up their friends. No husband keeps female friends and no wife I know of keeps any male friends, if she had any in the first place. Hardly makes it worthwhile." She looked slyly at Marianne. "Besides,

I don't believe the 'friend' bit and neither do the social columns. Have you seen the latest *World*?"

Marianne looked puzzled. She occasionally read the Society papers upon her mother's recommendation that she keep up with the goings-on about Town, but she hadn't gotten into the habit of reading them daily. She had, however, met some ladies who waited earnestly for the new editions to arrive.

Roberta dug into the reticule she carried. "I clipped this out for you, in case you hadn't seen it." She handed Marianne a small piece of newsprint.

Marianne scanned the little scrap of paper. Such a scrap shouldn't matter so much. But it did. The suggestions were horrifying. Against the backdrop of Alasdair's engagement to another, the insinuation that he was after Marianne's money and possibly willing to jilt another for it was positively lurid. Roberta was studying her intently, waiting for a reaction. Marianne carefully schooled her features, forcing them into blandness in order to not give herself away.

"I felt you should know," Roberta said with a sincerity Marianne didn't quite believe. Instinctively, something about Roberta bothered Marianne, compelling her to believe this "bosom-bow" act was just that. Marianne was convinced that Roberta hadn't told her this news out of a genuine desire to protect a friend; they didn't know each other well enough for such confidences. There was another reason, a hidden reason, for these disclosures; and yet, whatever her reason for sharing these things, it didn't make the items untrue. The article in the paper wasn't a fabrication. It had been printed and read by countless people.

Marianne felt panic rising, memories of New York springing forth. She wouldn't let it happen again. She desperately wanted to get away from Roberta, but Roberta was prosing on now about the merits of her cousin, Kentworth. Marianne relaxed only slightly. Roberta's ploy to advocate for her cousin was hardly subtle.

"Quick, put that away. He's coming over here," Roberta whispered in a rush as she suddenly broke from her conversation topic and gestured to the scrap of paper Marianne still held in her hand.

Marianne looked up to see Alasdair striding toward them, combed and confident, turned out resplendently in dark evening attire. In spite of Roberta's news, Marianne felt only relief at the sight of Alasdair even though he couldn't possibly know that he was coming to her rescue.

Alasdair greeted them and Roberta slipped into the crowd of people merging toward their seats. "Is she a new friend?" Alasdair asked, taking her by the elbow and steering her into the throng.

"I'm not sure. She and her mother have called a few times at our at homes but I'm not sure she's a friend in the truest sense. I would hardly call her more than an acquaintance." Marianne flicked her gaze up to Alasdair's face. It was hard to believe all of Roberta's information when he looked so at ease, so friendly. Standing so close to him now, she could smell the clean scent of his cologne. She'd thought he liked her. She couldn't be so completely wrong in her original assumptions. She was usually a good judge of character, but she'd been wrong about the girls in New York. Perhaps she was wrong about Alasdair too.

"What is it, Marianne?" Alasdair asked quietly. "You seem troubled."

She wanted to blurt everything out. He seemed so kind, so honest. She wanted to ask him about Sarah Stewart but that would only be shrewish and she had no claims on him to ask something so personal. Instead, she said, "Roberta showed me the article in the *World*."

Alasdair squeezed her elbow in reassurance. "I saw it too. I am sorry for it. It's entirely my fault. I wasn't as careful as I should have been." He gave her a flirting smile that melted her heart even as his words melted her hopes that Roberta had been wrong. She knew what he meant now that Roberta had explained it all. He should have been more careful because he was promised to another.

"Where are we going?" Marianne queried, suddenly aware they'd passed rows and rows of chairs and were making their way toward the front of the ballroom.

"I've got seats for us close to the stage. Camberly insisted we all sit up front and support his wife. I've already shown your parents. They should be waiting for us. Camberly is thrilled to hear about your father's new yacht. The two of them will talk of nothing else all night, I guarantee." Alasdair winked and Marianne couldn't help but laugh.

Roberta might be right about some things but she was wrong about others. Men and women could be friends. Marianne liked to think she and Alasdair were fast becoming proof of that. She took her seat, some of her concern eased. Camberly leaned past her father to acknowledge her arrival with a nod. She was smart enough to know that Alasdair wouldn't have invited her to sit with Camberly if he didn't like her. He had no obligations to her and yet he'd elected to include her in his elite group of friends.

Alasdair shifted in his seat. The program was a little over halfway done, Audrey had yet to play, and he was already fidgety in the tiny chair. These folding seats weren't made for taller men. He wondered how Camberly and Lionel tolerated it. They managed to look moderately comfortable and engaged. But they didn't have Marianne Addison sitting next to them, vibrating with energy.

He'd hoped to arrive in time to speak with her about the article. He'd hoped to be the one to tell her about it. He'd not wanted her to hear of it from another. He could imagine the speculations running through her mind. How did this all look to her? Did she think he was only paying homage to her fortune? But he'd been delayed by his mother, who had insisted that he drop her off at another entertainment before he came on to this one.

At least Marianne had not accused him of fortune hunting. In fact, he was heartened that she'd been quite polite, almost relieved, to see him. Still, he wanted to whisk her out of the room and go someplace private where they could talk, where he could explain the falsities of the article and his true intentions, whatever those intentions were.

He was having difficulty explaining those intentions to himself, let alone to his close friends. He knew only that the longer he was with Marianne, the more he wanted to be with her.

Part of him felt like quite the parasite: he was more than willing to bask in the glow of Marianne's smile, her joy in living, her confidence in doing what she wanted to do, and he was happy to live off of her contagious good spirits. It was those good spirits he'd vowed to protect from Brantley and his ilk. He didn't want Marianne to be changed so much by London that she was no longer herself. Neither did he want to see her pay the price for being that unique entity.

He snatched a glance at her in profile, taking in the pert snub of her nose and the graceful sweep of her jaw from chin to ear. Pearl earbobs hung delicately from those ears. It was tempting to touch the dangling pearl with a gentle push of a finger. He might have given in to that temptation if she hadn't chosen that moment to catch him staring.

"You're not paying attention. The countess is going to play next," Marianne whispered. Her breath was fresh, smelling of peppermint leaves. The urge to stand up and walk out of the room with her was nearly overpowering.

"I don't think I've ever sat next to someone so lovely before," Alasdair whispered glibly. But the words didn't do his sentiments justice. He wanted to touch her, connect to her in some vital way before he went insane with wanting.

Alasdair noted that a length of her gauzy wrap had dropped into the tiny space between their chairs. Around them, people applauded the musicians who'd finished their string piece. Unnoticed, Alasdair reached to retrieve the material, placing the tail of the wrap in her lap. "It was on the floor—I didn't want to see it stepped on or ruined," he said by way of explanation when Marianne sent him a querying look.

"Thank you. I hadn't noticed." Marianne blushed, a delightful rose hue staining her cheeks. It was all the proof he needed that she'd noticed he hadn't removed his hand. Instead, his hand remained discreetly hidden beneath the retrieved fabric, lightly curled over hers. He gave her gloved hand a squeeze. He shot her a sideways glance. Her eyes were dutifully fixed on the Countess of Camberly taking her place at the piano bench, but beneath the fabric Alasdair felt Marianne squeeze back.

He could not hold back the smile that lit his face. He just might be on the brink of that very dangerous precipice where a man teeters right before he falls in love.

The card room at the Radcliffes' was technically empty. All but one man had managed to drift into the ballroom to hear the renowned countess play a Schubert piece. A second figure, this one female, stole into the room, casting furtive glances behind her at the door for fear of being caught.

"There's no need for such antics. Everyone wants to hear the countess play, goodness knows why. I don't see why Camberly lets her get away with a career." Brantley was sprawled on a sofa, brandy in hand, his tone bored. He idly swirled the brandy in the snifter. "Did you give the article to Miss Addison?"

The young woman nodded. "She hadn't seen it." There was an overt touch of malice to her voice.

Brantley gave the girl a sardonic smile. "I hope you commiserated appropriately with her?"

She nodded, encouraged by Brantley's comment. "Of course. I don't think Miss Addison was too pleased to hear that the viscount was promised to another, either. I could tell she didn't know what to make of that."

"You've done well, Roberta." Brantley rose from the sofa and moved toward her. "We'll need to get Pennington's engagement to Sarah Stewart mentioned more publicly, or at least hinted at in the social columns, to remind people of his prior commitment. It would reflect poorly on our Miss Addison if she were stealing another girl's intended." Brantley made a mock moue.

Roberta gave a slight pout. "What about me? I want to be mentioned in the columns. You said you'd get me noticed if I did this for you."

Brantley tipped her chin up with his forefinger. "You'll be mentioned in the right way, my dear. Not all mentions are positive press. I wouldn't want your reputation tainted before we can announce our own engagement. You understand, of course?"

Roberta beamed. "I understand perfectly. It's so good of you to look out for me."

"Now, back to the party. I don't want anyone to miss you unduly." Brantley dismissed her, his thoughts already leaping ahead to the next part in his campaign to make the Viscount Pennington very sorry he had ever contrived to spill champagne on him.

If all went as planned, Brantley wouldn't be marrying the pretty but petty Miss Farnwick. He'd be marrying the American heiress. Desperate girls often did desperate things, and when he got done with the viscount, she would be very desperate indeed. There was no getting around it: in order to get to the viscount, Miss Addison would have to be sacrificed.

Chapter Six

Marianne strolled along the packed gravel path of the garden behind the town house. This morning, she appreciated the absolute luxury of their rented home. Only the older Mayfair homes could boast gracious, open garden spaces and deep horseshoe-shaped drives where a carriage could pull in to drop off passengers. There simply wasn't anywhere left to build. Newer townhomes were constructed right on the street's edge. The solitude provided by the high hedges and fences of the garden blocked out the street noise, effectively leaving her alone with her thoughts.

Those thoughts were riotous and confusing. She'd preferred to have sorted through them with her hands immersed in sourdough, but she'd quickly been banned from the kitchen the last time she'd tried it. The cook that came with the house was as uppity as Snead the butler. Everyone had their place and Marianne's place was *not* the kitchen. The garden would have to do.

Marianne absently fingered the soft petals of a rosebush, the flowers' silky texture reminding her of Alasdair's hand on hers during the recital. She knew she was re-creating something of a fantasy. Their hands had been gloved, and with the barriers of cloth between them there'd hardly been any real contact. But it was the gesture that had mattered more than the realities of the situation. The gesture was not the action of a friend—it was far too risky for that. Friends did not defy protocol and flirt with scandal to hold hands, no matter how discreetly, in a place as public as a recital hall or ballroom. No, the gesture itself was the act of an ardent suitor, undeclared though he was.

Was that what Alasdair was? An ardent suitor? The thought brought a halt to her absent caress of the rose petals. This was where things became confusing. He could not be a legitimate suitor if his affections were engaged elsewhere. His actions last night did not speak well of him if indeed there was a fiancée tucked away in the country. It was quite deflating to think of Alasdair in terms of his being a rake, wooing one woman while bound to another.

Marianne knew there were men like that, but she'd perceived Alasdair to be above such behavior. It was even worse to think of Alasdair against the backdrop of the horrid news clipping, to think that he was wooing her for her fortune and that he would contemplate throwing over his intended for the sake of a larger dowry.

She was further troubled to think that Alasdair may have pursued such a dubious course of action because he felt that neither of the women involved would find out. If Roberta Farnwick was to be believed, Miss Stewart never came up to Town. Likely, she was entirely unaware of her intended's behaviors when he was away. Marianne also knew herself to be an ideal candidate. She was new to Town and couldn't possibly know about the arrangement.

A stem snapped under the pressure of Marianne's hand. She looked down regretfully at the broken bloom. She'd not realized how much turmoil her thoughts had created until the flower had broken. Was this to be the measure of her days? Wandering the garden, picking apart every action, every nuance, trying to make a whole?

When she'd concocted her idea to come to England, it had all seemed so simple. She had planned for every contingency. The trip had been meticulously outlined over the course of the months before they had traveled. Appointments had been set at Worth, the big town house had been arranged, and apartments in Paris and Venice had been contracted for their short visits there. All the details had been firmly established right down to the first few vital invitations that Marianne's mother had networked for them through a friend of a friend.

In all of the planning, Marianne had not counted on a suitor like Alasdair Braden. In her planning, she'd imagined her suitors to be like young Kentworth, a decent-looking fellow closer to her own age, easily managed with a quick smile. While there were plenty of young men like Roberta's cousin who were happy to be part of her court, Alasdair was the only one who stood out. It wasn't that he was the only full-grown man—there were others in her little court who had reached the prime of their maturity—but none of them drew her like Alasdair.

Marianne stopped at a cluster of flowers and cut some to make a bouquet around the flower whose stem she'd ruined. Satisfied with her cuttings, she dropped them into the basket on her arm and continued her slow perambulations, assessing Alasdair.

Indeed, it seemed to her that no other man in London possessed his charm, not even the dashing Earl of Camberly. An extra sense told her when Alasdair was in the room. Her skin prickled at the very nearness of him. It had been hard work simply to sit beside him the night before and pay any attention to the fine music. The day he'd escorted them to Hatchards, she'd been acutely aware of his presence, the faint scent of his soap and morning toilet that clung appealingly to his skin and clothes. The smell was as complex as the man himself was proving to be.

Was Alasdair Braden another money-hungry peer or a genuinely ardent suitor who merely had the mishap of being surrounded by unpleasant gossip? Marianne knew about both. The newspapers in New York had made no attempt to dress up the reasons the Duke of Marlborough had been courting Consuelo Vanderbilt. She'd also experienced firsthand the power of rumors to define one's realities. She'd be the last one to try and pigeonhole Alasdair into any stereotypes. Still, it would be much easier to decide how best to respond to him if she knew the truth about him.

All of these speculations skirted the larger issue: What did she want from Alasdair? Did she want him to declare himself as a suitor? Marianne cut a vibrant magenta bloom from an azalea bush and pushed it behind her ear. What did it matter how indecorous it looked? There was no one to see. No one was expected today, which was just as well. She had too much to ponder. Her thoughts easily drifted back to Alasdair.

She was undeniably drawn to him, but it was safer thinking of him as a friend, no matter how American that notion appeared to be. Seeing London up close, firsthand, Marianne was starting to realize there were things for which she could not plan. The intricacies of life among London's peers was an entirely different culture. If she were to cast her lot with the aristocracy, she'd forever risk being a fish out of water. How would she learn to function as the titled wife of a viscount or earl? Marianne sat down on a stone bench on the edge of a gravel path. She began picking the lingering petals off of a wilting bloom.

The image she had of herself as a countess like Audrey St. Clair-Maddox would be humorous in some circumstances. She could imagine shocking the servants when she went below stairs to make bread. She could imagine horrifying the footmen when she fetched her own vase for flowers. She would laugh at giving them fits, but Alasdair wouldn't find that kind of woman amusing, at least not as a wife.

He would need someone who could command a battalion of servants, lay out immaculate dinner-seating charts and see that everyone got to the table in the right order of precedence without creating tomorrow's scandal. Marianne doubted she'd be capable of that, or that she'd *want* to devote herself so tirelessly to such behaviors that were, in her opinion, close to meaningless.

It simply wasn't in her. She had not understood that when she'd embarked on her impulsive campaign to snare an English title. There'd be a husband that went with it, and there'd be more than that. One man could be managed. But there would be families and traditions that went back far longer than her country had even been on the map.

Perhaps it would be enough to say she'd succeeded in London and to go home without a title. That should be enough to show the snobs in New York that they'd been wrong about her. It wasn't like her to quit, but she wasn't quitting. She'd stay in London and enjoy the Season. She would merely reshape her goal into something more practical. There was no sense in cutting off one's nose to spite one's face. In this situation, the old adage fit perfectly. She wasn't going to ruin her life by taking on a burden she didn't want just to show the New York nobs she hadn't deserved the cut direct.

Marianne stood up and brushed at her skirts. Her meanderings were getting out of hand. She hadn't even determined that she had a real suitor yet, and here she was already deciding to reject his marriage proposal. This must be what English girls on the marriage mart did all day since they were forbidden to do anything else.

She made her way back to the house, basket in hand filled with flowers to arrange, when she encountered the object of her morning ruminations. Alasdair was coming down the walk toward her, his stride wide and quick, his face lighting in a smile at the sight of her. Marianne remembered too late the azalea blossom tucked behind her ear. She left it there. She liked the sweet smell of it and that was all that mattered. If her ruminations had led her to any useful conclusions it was that she was Marianne Addison, and she could be no other.

"Your mother said I could find you out here." Alasdair took the basket from her arm. "I left the others inside."

"Others?" Marianne asked.

"Camberly and his wife, Carrington and Stella. It was such a lovely day that we decided to drive over and see if you were free. We've got an impromptu picnic arranged. Please say yes. I know it's short notice, but you'll adore Regent's Park. There's a lake for boating—more like a placid river, really—and Camberly is having the archery butts set up. He's got a silly competition with Carrington going on that I don't pretend to understand."

Alasdair was completely irresistible as he enumerated the benefits of a picnic. "Stop!" Marianne laughed, her earlier anxieties swept away in the wake of his boyish arguments. "You had me hooked at the first mention of a picnic. Give me a moment to change."

The picnic was unlike anything Marianne had ever attended. Camberly's servants had gone ahead of them and erected a three-sided pavilion at the park. Inside, a portable round table and folding chairs had been set up near a long sideboard holding an enormous quantity of food. The table itself was covered in white linen and china plates. On the other side of the pavilion was a small outdoor seating area with pillows and chaises for the ladies. "The better to watch our display of prowess at the archery butts," Lionel commented with a waggle of his fair eyebrows.

"Well, my prowess at least," Camberly joined in, helping Audrey down from the carriage. "I'm not sure about Lionel's."

Everyone laughed, and Marianne was overwhelmed

with a sense of belonging. She'd never had friends like these people before. They included her in all their activities as if she'd been one of them from the start. Clearly, they had all been together for ages. It was hard to imagine that Audrey had only joined their ranks a few years ago. The American who'd become a countess fit seamlessly among them.

Marianne felt a twinge of envy watching Lionel with Stella and the earl with Audrey. The earl had seemed relatively reserved at the social events where she'd seen him, but here, under the sunny skies of the park and with his wife on his arm, the earl was an entirely different man. It was all too easy to pretend that today she was Alasdair's and the group was a sextet of couples.

"Do you shoot, Miss Addison?" the earl asked once everyone had been settled to his satisfaction.

"Guns," she replied automatically.

Lionel laughed hysterically. "You deserved that, Camberly. Haven't you been around Americans long enough to know that archery isn't really our thing? We're all about guns, Camberly. Arrows aren't much use are they, Marianne, on the Barbary Coast?"

Realizing the earl's intended meaning, Marianne laughed too. "No, I'm afraid I don't do any archery," she said once the laughter subsided.

"What's the Barbary Coast?" Stella asked, looking around the group. "I am assuming we're not talking about pirates?"

Lionel drew a deep breath to calm his laughter. "It's

a rather unsavory section of town in San Francisco, where gambling hells, brothels, and all nature of vice is available. There are stories of men who go in to get a drink and that's the last anyone sees of them. Bartenders slip drugs into drinks and harlots slip money out of wallets while the clients are drugged. Some of them wake up on a ship bound for India or China. Others just wake up in a gutter."

Stella shuddered. "San Francisco sounds very dangerous. Is that why you're so handy with a gun, Miss Addison?"

"Call me Marianne, please." Marianne wanted to laugh at the very obvious divide between English and American behaviors among friends. Lionel had called her Marianne, but Camberly and Stella had clung to the formality of her last name.

"No, San Francisco is much changed from what it used to be. We have safety committees and organized groups that keep the town law-abiding. We even have churches," Marianne teased dryly. "I learned to shoot because I traveled with my father to Denver a few years ago and we stayed with some avid hunters. It seemed the thing to do."

"Well, when in Rome, one must do as the Romans do." Alasdair held out his hand to her. "Come with me and I'll show you how to 'shoot' English style. We've a long tradition of famous archers, you know. Robin Hood and all that." He winked. "You've heard of Robin Hood?" he said in mock seriousness.

Marianne swatted at him for good measure. "I know your Robin Hood, but in America we have Jim Bowie and Davy Crockett."

"Are they archers?" Alasdair asked, picking up a bow and testing it.

"No. Bowie was known for his knife work." Marianne grinned.

Alasdair gave an exaggerated sigh. "Then we have a lot of work to do." Everyone laughed and Marianne followed him out to the butts.

"This is Audrey's, so the weight should be fine for you," Alasdair said as he handed her a well-carved bow. "Pull back on the string and let's test it before we use an arrow."

Marianne held the bow flat out in front of her and pulled on the string only to have Alasdair say, "No, not like that. Lift it up to nearly shoulder level, as if you mean to shoot it. Like this."

In an instant, Alasdair had his arms about her, his hands on hers, guiding the bow into position and helping her to pull back the string. A tremor ran through her at his nearness. Up close, she could smell the exquisite mix of his soap: sage and thyme with a subdued hint of lavender and perhaps something else. She could feel his body pulse around her, the muscles of his arms drawn taut against her, proving that this man had the ability to mesh both the world of the drawing room and dance floor with the rigors of the outdoors.

Too soon, Alasdair stepped back from their instructive embrace. "I'll get an arrow" he murmured in a husky voice that suggested to Marianne that he was quite possibly as moved by the encounter as she was.

He took his time getting a few arrows and removing his coat before he returned to her side. When he did, all traces of huskiness were gone from his voice, making Marianne think perhaps she'd imagined it.

"The arrow fits like this," Alasdair aptly demonstrated. "Then we pull it back. That's called 'nocking' the arrow. And we let it loose." Alasdair closed one eye and sighted the target, hefting the bow and loosing the arrow in a single fluid motion. The arrow gave a soft thud as it hit the target. "Now you try it," Alasdair encouraged, passing the bow back to her.

Marianne did her best to copy Alasdair's movements, but nocking the arrow was harder than it looked. The arrow kept slipping.

"Here, let me help," Alasdair said gently, coming around her again and placing his hands over hers. Together, they let the arrow fly. It landed near the center of the target and Marianne clapped in delight. The next one she did on her own, thrilled that the arrow didn't slip even though it did miss most of the target, landing on the far edge of the butt.

Beside her, Alasdair handed her another arrow. "Keep trying—you're getting it."

She smiled and attempted to concentrate. After a

few more shots, she was able to hit the target more respectably. The little group in the pavilion applauded her last effort before Audrey called them over for lunch.

Camberly opened a bottle of champagne and everyone assembled plates of cold chicken, strawberries and other summer delicacies before sitting down at the table. "We must have a toast," he said, still standing. "To Miss Addison. Here's to the addition of another fabulous American among us."

Glasses clinked, and while Marianne was moved by the gesture, and indeed by all the kindnesses the group had shown her, she couldn't help but wonder why they had befriended her. Watching her father do business over the years, Marianne had learned that no one did anything without reason.

Across the table, Alasdair gave her a warm smile. She'd like to believe that they'd invited her into their group simply because Alasdair was courting her. But since she wasn't even sure he was courting her or that he was in any position to be courting her, she could hardly draw any further conclusions.

After lunch, the men suggested a row on the little river that ran through the park, to give the servants time to clean up from the meal. Alasdair offered his arm to her for the short walk to the boat shed, and once again Marianne was struck by how right it felt to be a third couple among the group.

"Are you having a good time?" Alasdair inquired, slowing their pace a bit to drop behind the group.

Marianne looked up at him from under the brim of her hat. "I'm having a lovely time. Do you doubt it?"

"No, I can see it in your face, dear Marianne. That's one of the things I love about you—all the things you feel are written clearly there. There's no artifice." The last was said with such seriousness that Marianne almost stopped walking altogether. There was too much embedded in that statement to let it pass unaddressed. She supposed she could ignore the somber undertones of the message and offer a flirtatious reply, such as 'What else do you love about me?' but Marianne opted for plain speaking. Now, she did stop walking.

She fixed Alasdair with her strong blue gaze, letting him see that this was no flirtatious rejoinder. "Alasdair, what are you doing?"

To his immense credit, he understood precisely what she meant. He lifted one of her hands to his lips and pressed a kiss on it, his eyes unwaveringly holding her gaze until Marianne feared she'd be the one to look away first from the intensity of the moment. No moment in her life to date had ever been this intimate, this powerful. "Why, Marianne, I thought it was abundantly clear," Alasdair replied in a quiet voice intended for her ears only. "I am courting you."

Chapter Seven

Two days ago, Marianne would have accepted his statement with equanimity and with gratitude that the mystery of Alasdair's intentions was resolved. Now, the burden of Roberta's gossip and the knowledge that Alasdair had an understanding with another marred the straightforward reaction she might otherwise have had. How was she to respond?

Marianne let Alasdair hand her into the rowboat. The others were already launched into the current of the man-made stream. Marianne was thankful for the privacy their absence afforded them and for Alasdair's silence. He plied the oars in quiet, giving her time to think.

"Have I been too precipitous?" Alasdair asked casually, laying the oars in their locks and letting the current gently take the boat. He leaned forward, elbows on his knees, the breeze blowing his hair in a boyish fashion that lent him an earnest quality.

"You do me a great honor with your attentions," Marianne began, surprised to see Alasdair start to laugh.

"Stop right there. That's what girls say when they're about to reject a suitor."

Marianne arched her eyebrows in query. "You've been rejected a lot then?" She laughed too. Her words were entirely too inane by half. They deserved no less than the laughter with which Alasdair was responding to them. She shrugged helplessly. "In my defense, it's what they teach young ladies to say when they don't know what to say."

Alasdair stopped laughing. "Why is that, Marianne? I thought we were becoming good friends—more than friends, I hoped."

It was Marianne's turn to sober. No would-be suitor had ever been so frank with her. Alasdair deserved complete honesty in return. She met his gaze with a businesslike look. "I've been told that you're promised to another." She held her breath. Would he deny it? She stripped off her glove and trailed her hand in the water, trying to pretend his answer didn't matter when in reality it seemed everything hinged on it. Perhaps everything did. His reply would answer much about his character and his intentions. No man of honor, from the basest San Francisco wharf worker to a highborn aristocrat, would court one woman while committed to another.

Alasdair nodded slowly. "So you've heard the rumors. They're true as far as rumors go." They'd drifted toward the park side of the stream. He set himself to the oars again, steering them back to the middle of the stream.

Marianne's world slowed. She was overconscious of the play of his muscles beneath his shirt while he rowed, all too aware of his dark eyes watching her, gauging her reaction. She would have to let him go. There was no choice. Perhaps she'd been wrong all along. Men and women could not be friends. She saw in startling clarity how she could not tolerate merely being Alasdair's friend, standing aside while he paid romantic homage to another. Alasdair was speaking again, his voice forcing its way into her bleak thoughts.

"My mother has hopes that I'll offer for a neighbor's daughter. She's made those hopes fairly public, but those hopes have no claim on me. There is nothing more that binds me to Miss Stewart—no legal contract, no betrothal ceremony. I have informed my mother that I have no intentions of marrying Miss Stewart."

"And your intentions toward me?" Marianne pressed warily.

"I like you, Marianne, a great deal," Alasdair said solemnly. "I think you like me too. It makes sense that we should follow that premise to its logical conclusion and discover if we suit one another."

All the objections Marianne had sorted through in the garden that morning came roaring back. "What would that logical conclusion be? You can't really believe I'd be an adequate countess."

The boat rounded a quiet bend in the stream out of view of the shoreline. Alasdair leaned on the oars, putting himself just inches from her. "Don't you think we deserve a chance to find out? I'm a man who believes the future takes care of itself as long as we get our jobs done in the present. Right now, I just want to kiss you," he whispered, and he closed the small gap between them and did precisely that.

The kiss was chaste as kisses went, the pressure of his lips lasting no more than fleeting seconds. Nonetheless, the kiss spoke of promises implied, and Marianne knew that she would savor this kiss always, regardless of the outcome. She'd been kissed a few times before—mistletoe games at Christmas parties and once in an encounter with the son from a rich San Francisco family who desired an alliance with the Addison baking industry. None of those kisses equaled Alasdair's in intent or intensity. This was her first real kiss, a kiss that meant *something*.

Alasdair leaned back, putting distance between them. The boat had sailed into view of the shoreline. Soon, they'd be caught up with the others.

"You still haven't answered my question, Marianne."

She smiled impishly, more certain of her response now that certain issues that been settled between them. "I don't recall that it was precisely a question," she bantered. "I believe you stated unequivocally that you were courting me."

"Does that meet with your approval?" Alasdair rejoined.

"I think we should carry things to their logical conclusion and find out."

Alasdair laughed. "How very scientific of you, my dear."

The remainder of the afternoon was devoted to Camberly and Lionel's good-natured archery contest. Alasdair stood with the two men, offering bits of advice and ribbing. From the comfort of the chaise longues, where she sat with the other two women, Marianne studied Alasdair with covert glances, marveling at his composure. Her insides were topsy-turvy, her mind replaying each sentence and word of their conversation, pausing at the kiss. She was realizing the problem with kisses: one was hardly enough. She wanted another. Would the next kiss be as wondrous as the first or was that kiss the rarest of things, singular in its existence?

"Marianne, did you hear me?" Audrey asked politely, a knowing smile softly lighting her features. "Stella, I think she's quite infatuated with our Alasdair."

Marianne blushed and stammered an incoherent

apology that Audrey waved away with an elegant gesture. "There's no need to apologize, my dear. We've both felt that way before. Not with Alasdair, of course," she added hastily.

Stella shaded her eyes against the sun and gave Alasdair a considering look. "He's handsome enough for a dark-haired man. I prefer the blond ones myself." She and Audrey laughed together over her joke. At the archery butts, Lionel's pale blond hair was a marked contrast to the two dark-haired men with whom he stood.

A thousand questions competed for attention in Marianne's head. These two women were among Alasdair's acquaintances. Was it wrong to make inquiries about a suitor among his friends? She had to admit that part of her found something secretive and dishonest about seeking information that way. Curiosity won out. Surely if she limited her questions to the basics, there would be no harm. "Have you known Alasdair long?" That would definitely be a safe question.

Audrey took pity on her. The countess leaned forward and placed a hand on her arm. "I've only known Alasdair since my marriage, but my husband swears he's the best of friends. Alasdair may be impulsive but he's not dishonorable."

Stella broke in. "If you're wondering if he's a proper suitor, you can lay your worries to rest."

"It's just that it has all happened so quickly," Marianne replied, leaning back on the cushions of her chaise longue. For all the questions she was tempted to ask, she found herself quite loath to ask them aloud. The ones that mattered most were the ones that politeness required they remain unasked. She could not ask his friends if the size of her fortune hastened his intentions.

It hardly mattered. From what she'd observed about the unfailing politeness of the English, no one would honestly answer that question. She could not bear the idea that Alasdair's affections could be bought or that the kiss they'd shared on the boat had been an indicator of his appreciation for her money instead of his appreciation for her. Marianne also realized that she might not have been so acutely aware of the issue if the social columns had not singled out the topic as their justification for Alasdair's attentions.

She needed to concentrate on keeping it all in perspective. But doubt was a hard enemy to fight, and wasn't she better off knowing about his needs for funds from the first? She tried to convince herself that it would be far worse to discover his financial situation later, perhaps even at a point where there was no turning back, no choices. It would be beyond humiliating to lose one's heart to a man who loved nothing about you but your dollars even though you'd fallen madly in love with him.

She wasn't madly in love with Alasdair yet, she promised herself. But she could be all too easily. A handsome man bound with muscles and manners was not easy to resist. If the feelings were mutual, why re-sist at all? If the feelings were one-sided and motivated by greed on the other, it would be best to get out before one was further engaged. In that scenario, there would be no happily-ever-after, only misery for the one who'd loved foolishly.

Marianne knew herself well enough to know that she couldn't tolerate an arrangement of such half-truths and pretenses of affection. She lived out loud and she highly suspected she would love that way, too, when the time came.

The afternoon shadows lengthened and the archery competition came to an end, bringing the men back into the open pavilion, laughing. It was time to head home. Around her, Marianne noticed servants discreetly pack-ing the wagon with items no longer in use.

"We stayed longer than I thought," Audrey said, ris-ing from her chaise with a yawn. "Forgive us, Mari-anne. I hope you aren't rushed with your evening preparations. We still have the carriage trip home and the streets will be crowded at this hour."

"There's no rush. We are dining at home tonight be-fore attending the theater," Marianne said.

"We'll be there too," Camberly put in, rolling down his sleeves and shrugging into his jacket with Audrey's help. "Perhaps you'll consider joining us in our box? It will just be the five of us. There's plenty of room for you and your parents."

Last night it had been front row seats at the musicale,

today a private picnic in the park and box seats at the opera. The thought fleetingly crossed Marianne's mind that all the benefits of what a life with Alasdair could bring were on not-so-subtle display. Even a viscount with financial concerns led an elite life. Then again, the offer might be nothing more than Camberly's kindness. She preferred to think the latter was true.

Everyone piled into the carriages and they began the slow drive back to Mayfair. Alasdair jumped down and escorted her to the door, his hand resting lightly at the small of her back, a wondrously intimate touch yet publicly acceptable.

"Until tonight, Marianne." Alasdair bowed over her hand, brushing her gloved knuckles with his lips.

"I will look forward to it. You must thank Camberly again for his invitation." Marianne smiled, doing her best to mask her thoughts. But as she slipped inside the house, she couldn't help contemplating the old adage: "When it sounds too good to be true, then it probably is."

The theater was filled to capacity and noise reached the level of a thundering roar, but movement in the Earl of Camberly's box drew Brantley's attention from his seat in the stalls. He scanned the box with his opera glasses. The usual suspects were there, including that dratted Pennington and the American chit. It appeared she'd even brought her parents along, a sure sign that things were progressing in a serious direction.

Pennington seated the girl and her parents in the front row of the box and took a chair next to her. The act was gallantly polite on Pennington's part but it also unintentionally offered Brantley a full look at the heiress. By God, the girl was lovely, all of that beautiful soft gold hair intricately piled on top of her head. She turned to speak with the man behind her, revealing the exquisite curve of her jaw. Brantley thought it would be no hardship wedding her and her fortune even if she wasn't English. He could do far worse and he was in no position to be picky. Beside her, Pennington laughed at something she said. Brantley frowned. The handsome viscount was welcome to charm her all he liked, because in the end, it wouldn't matter.

The lights went down. Alasdair reached for Marianne's hand where it lay in her lap. He didn't care what was happening on stage. He only cared that the dim lights allowed him the ability to touch Marianne, to make a physical connection with her. After the picnic today, he'd known without doubt that he'd never been drawn to another the way he was drawn to her. She was all laughter and light, and yet shrewd, always assessing a situation. He had no doubts about her virtue, yet she was refreshingly blunt.

It was the American gift, he supposed. English-women who possessed such forthrightness were usually not also in possession of a virtuous lifestyle. But

American girls avoided that trap. Audrey had explained to him that American girls didn't waste away in schoolrooms until their debuts. They sat at dinner tables with their parents and conversed with adults as if they were adults themselves, voicing their opinions to an eager audience that encouraged free speaking at an early age.

Marianne had certainly benefited from such an education. Perhaps it was that very same education which created her vivacity and lent her the air of confidence that perpetually surrounded her. Even today, when she'd been unsure of her course in the boat, she'd kept her wits and questioned him. Alasdair could not have admired her more than he had at that moment in the boat when she'd looked him in the eye and asked him his intentions. More girls might benefit from such behavior. Too bad there wasn't a guidebook for debutantes that suggested such a thing.

Marianne squeezed his hand and shot him an impish look he could barely make out in the dimness of the box, but it was acknowledgment enough of their secret—hands trysting in the dark. He'd prefer kissing her again but he could hardly step out into the corridor with her and engage in such flagrant behavior.

Besides, purloined kisses weren't what he wanted from her. The kiss that afternoon had been brief by necessity. He wanted more than that. He wanted kisses that lingered, that explored, that weren't rushed because social convention demanded that they not occur at all. It was ridiculous that even the quick peck he'd stolen was considered out-of-bounds. No wonder a plethora of married couples ended up unhappy. They hardly knew each other in the ways that mattered.

Property lines and finances were not enough on which to build a marriage, at least not the type of marriage to which he aspired. He wished he could make his mother understand that. Alasdair understood that his dilemma was not a new one. The aristocracy had long been plagued with the dichotomy of marrying for love or for money. He rather hoped that in Marianne he'd found the perfect solution to combine both.

The curtains went down and the lights went up, signaling the intermission. Alasdair quickly disengaged his hand from Marianne's and rose. As always, the Camberly box was immediately swarmed by acquaintances and friends. Tonight, many of them were eager to meet Marianne. Alasdair was happy to give her over to Audrey and watch her at a distance until Brantley's perpetually bored, nasal tones demanded his attention.

"She's a lovely girl, Pennington. Quite striking, if you ask me. Introduce me, Pennington. A belated introduction is better than none at all. You owe me that, at least."

Alasdair had no choice. It would be the height of rudeness not to make the introduction, and to refuse might heighten Brantley's determination. Alasdair knew that if he protested too much Brantley would guess aright that more than money was engaged. Such knowledge would be a powerful weapon in Brantley's hands.

"Miss Addison." Alasdair broke into the small group of people with whom Marianne stood. "This is Lord Brantley. I believe you've only met briefly before."

In her characteristic fashion, Marianne extended her gloved hand to shake his. "I am charmed, my lord. I've heard your name before, haven't I?" she mused aloud. "Oh yes, now I remember. Pennington spilled your champagne. We were supposed to dance."

"Yes, he got the jump on me, I daresay. If I'd known what a delightful partner I was missing out on, I would have danced in a wet shirt. Perhaps I might be fortunate enough to claim another dance in place of the one we missed." Brantley was all smooth manners. Alasdair's eyes narrowed. In evening clothes with his blond hair combed neatly, the man might easily be mistaken for the gentleman he claimed he was.

"The second act is about to begin," Alasdair quickly interceded. The last thing he wanted was for Marianne to dance with this scoundrel. Brantley would not play fairly when it came to winning his bet. All it would take would be one short walk on a verandah after a dance and Brantley would not hesitate to compromise Marianne. The damage would be done.

As the overture started and people took their seats, Camberly leaned close to speak in low, private tones. "I think you should tell Marianne about the bet. Brantley has thrown down the gauntlet tonight. He approached her directly. She needs to know his intentions."

Alasdair nodded and sighed. He accepted the wisdom of Camberly's advice but that didn't mean he liked it. Courting Marianne was becoming a difficult ambition and she hadn't even met his mother yet.

Chapter Eight

Dressed in a smart walking ensemble of pale blue gabardine, Marianne strolled beside Alasdair the next morning, trying to look at everything around her without appearing to be overeager. Alasdair was showing them the sights of London, starting with the Tower. On his other side, her mother made polite comments while Alasdair pointed out various points of interest.

Marianne was enjoying herself immensely. She'd been surprised to learn that the Tower of London wasn't a tower in the strictest sense at all, but a large fortress sitting on the banks of the Thames in view of the Tower Bridge. It was early in the day yet for the bulk of sightseers, and the three of them virtually had the place to themselves. Marianne appreciated the peace and quiet. The Season was proving to be as exciting as she'd thought it would be, with all its parties and entertainments, but she was discovering just how wearing it could be to be surrounded by crowds of people and the din of their conversation on a constant basis.

Today at the Tower, there was plenty of space around them as they moved from sight to sight and there was plenty of quiet. The morning was comfortably cool, the sky blue overhead. Best of all, she had Alasdair to herself, or at least as much to herself as she could expect. While they were sightseeing, there were no limits to their time together, unlike when they were both in attendance at the balls and routs, where she could not dance more than twice with Alasdair the entire evening, or at the theater where they'd been among a large group.

Alasdair was an adept tour guide. "Sir Walter Raleigh's chambers are up those stairs. He spent a significant portion of his life there. Would you like to see them?"

"The same Walter Raleigh who is credited with discovering North Carolina?" Marianne's mother asked with interest.

"The very same." Alasdair motioned them on ahead of him through the narrow doorway. The chambers were not impossible living quarters, Marianne noted. They were certainly not anything akin to her dark imaginings of a prison cell. There was a wide fireplace, a sitting room big enough to receive guests, a place to work, and a bedchamber.

Marianne ran her fingers over the dark wood of a long table made smooth over time. "He had a window. He could see the river."

"You sound surprised." Alasdair came up behind her, leaving her mother to explore the bedchamber.

"It's not what I thought a prison would look like," Marianne confessed.

"Oh, we have other dank holes, I assure you. I'm convinced Newgate is one of the most barbarous places on the planet," Alasdair said in a cavalier tone.

But Marianne was in a more thoughtful mood and did not return his banter. She stared out the window, watching a boat head toward the mouth of the Thames. "I wonder if, living in these surroundings with at least some creature comforts, Sir Walter Raleigh didn't really believe the queen would have him executed."

"For all the luxury he may have had in these chambers, he still didn't have his freedom." Alasdair's voice carried a subtle undertone to it that caused Marianne to turn from the window.

He'd sounded so cavalier the previous moment, the haunted tone surprised her. The Alasdair she'd come to know in the past two weeks was a carefree man, unfettered by the world. His tone now suggested otherwise. The shadow in his dark eyes, which until now had only sparked with mischief and laughter, hinted that he knew the lure of freedom and the agony of living without it. She would not have guessed that a man like Alasdair would relate so strongly to the situation of Sir Walter Raleigh.

"Prisons are not made of walls alone," Alasdair said, looking past her to the small window.

His words moved her and touched something primal at her mind's core. Unmindful of anyone who might happen upon them, Marianne raised a gloved hand to his cheek. "I cannot conceive of a prison that could hold you if you did not wish it," she said softly.

Something Marianne could not define moved in Alasdair's eyes, the shadow receding to be replaced by a warmer look. He took her hand where it rested against his cheek and brought it to his lips to kiss in a smooth gesture. "Perhaps that is why I've come to cherish you so dearly, Marianne." He held her eyes over her hand. "I admire in you that which I don't possess myself. You are sunshine and lightness, the pure embodiment of all that is bold and good in this world." His voice was low, husky with intense emotion.

Marianne's own voice was hardly more than a trembling whisper. "What prison holds you, Alasdair? Surely one must, if you think so highly of me, for I fear that pedestal is one from which the fall would be too great."

"I would not darken your light with my burdens, Marianne. My burdens are no different than anyone else's of my station."

Marianne opened her mouth to coax more from him,

but her mother's return to the room preempted the opportunity. In any case, one glance at Alasdair revealed that the moment was gone. He was smiling, offering his arm to her mother and already chatting about the next spot of interest. His performance was so convincing, Marianne was hard-pressed to believe their intimate moment had even occurred. The threesome exited the room and Marianne cast a last look backward, imprinting on her mind the spot by the window. She wanted to remember that moment always; never had anyone shared so deeply with her.

She would treasure each word, each idea. She would remember both Alasdair's confession of inner turmoil *and* his confession of feelings for her. It put an undeniable spring her step, when they moved on to the Jewel House, that the handsome man beside her thought of her as sunshine and light. But she'd meant it, too, when she'd said such a pedestal was too high. She wasn't sure she deserved such adulation. She had burdens and secrets too, although they were no doubt of a different nature than the darker burdens he professed to carry.

Still, they were secrets for a reason. If it were up to her, she'd much prefer Alasdair not hear about her experience in New York. Apparently the Countess of Camberly felt the same way, since she'd not brought up the event in New York at all. Marianne was thankful for the countess' discretion. Perhaps the countess believed as she did—that it didn't seem fair for a single event of little account to affect the rest of one's life.

The rest of the Tower passed quickly. They took in the armory and the tragic White Tower. The place was filling with more visitors when they decided to leave. Marianne was happy to get away from the growing crowd. The bustle of groups being herded from spot to spot would diminish her experience. Marianne hugged her remembrances to herself all the way home in the open carriage and all through changing her gown for an afternoon ladies' tea at Mrs. John Mackay's.

Mrs. Mackay's well-earned reputation as a premier London hostess over the last decade did not disappoint. Her elegantly appointed town house contained a rare garden in Town, a garden that was large enough to host a tea. This afternoon, white canopies dotted the space. Tea tables and chairs for groups of eight were set beneath them, adorned in white cloths and vases of pink rosebuds. Even the weather conspired to assist in creating an ideal setting.

Quite unintentionally, Marianne had chosen the perfect dress for the occasion: a white dress of Egyptian cotton trimmed in pink silk ribbon at the hem and full falls of lace that reached her elbow-length gloves from her puffed sleeves. Her mother beamed proudly at her from across the table. "London agrees with you, Marianne."

"Or perhaps it's the Viscount Pennington," one young debutante sitting at the table offered with a giggle she quickly stifled after a not-so-subtle pinch from her mother.

"Are we talking about Pennington?" a familiar voice

said, stepping into the canopied area from the gravel path.

Marianne immediately recognized Roberta Farnwick and her mother. She exchanged polite pleasantries with them, hiding her dismay that they were seated with them. She had not seen Roberta since the Radcliffe musicale and she did not relish the idea of discussing anything about Alasdair with her after the last time she had done so.

Their hostess, Mrs. Mackay, passed by the table to inquire after their comfort, lingering long enough to exclaim over Marianne's gown.

"Louise Mackay is an enormous success story about overcoming scandal," Roberta's mother, Constance Farnwick, said with a knowledgeable air as she flipped open a black-lacquer fan with an Oriental design painted on its panels. She was a stylish woman with a worldly quality to her, tall and well dressed, yet she was not a friendly woman. Marianne could not imagine dissembling to her.

The others at the table leaned forward, interested. The statement was surely a prelude to a much larger on dit. A few of the older women at the table nodded their heads. Apparently the news wasn't all that fresh. Still, it was clear from the expectant looks on everyone's faces that even old gossip carried a certain thrilling cachet to it.

"You wouldn't know, of course, Miss Addison,

being new to London." Constance offered her and her mother a smile that managed to be both benevolent and condescending at once. "Mrs. Mackay used to live in a Nevada mining town. She made money by giving piano lessons, although some say she gave more than music instruction." She looked meaningfully around the table to reinforce her barely veiled implications. "She's what we call a woman who has 'translated' herself quite well into London society."

Marianne shot her mother a look. Was there a double meaning there? Had Mrs. Farnwick meant to suggest that the Addisons would need to "translate" themselves, as well, or was Mrs. Farnwick exhibiting excessively bad form in gossiping about their hostess?

Her mother returned her questioning look with a quiet smile before turning her attention to Mrs. Farnwick. "She should be applauded for her successes if they make her happy. Life in a mining town can be most difficult." Elizabeth Addison raised a hand to gesture to the grand garden about them. "Who has more right to make oneself over than the individuals themselves? No one has to live with our choices but us." Marianne silently applauded her mother's calm tenacity. Never, in her knowledge, had Marianne known her mother to let a slight to another stand when it was in her power to correct it.

"And our husbands," Mrs. Farnwick retorted, unwilling to lose the center of the group's attention.

"Mr. Mackay was reported, last year, to have punched a Charles Bonynge in the nose, in the middle of a bank, for maligning his wife's honor."

"A ghastly sign of the times." A woman Marianne did not know sighed heavily over her tea cup.

"Why is that?" Marianne asked.

The woman looked startled. She had not expected anyone to question her comment. "Why? My dear girl, a decent wifely candidate does not have to be defended against malicious rumors because she doesn't bring any questionable experiences into the marriage."

Another woman added her voice to the conversation. "It's all changing now that the queen doesn't rein in the prince. The prince tolerates all nature of entertainments. Even Mrs. Mackay can claim him on her guest lists. It's all about entertainment and money these days. It's all very gauche how our young men feel compelled to sell themselves to the highest bidder in order to keep their estates running." The woman feigned a shudder that rocked the feathers on her wide-brimmed hat.

Marianne let the comment pass. Surely whatever innuendo might be implied, it wasn't aimed at her or Alasdair. But the void in the conversation left the perfect opportunity for Roberta to jump in.

"There was even speculation a few days ago that Pennington's interest in our dear Miss Addison was merely based on her fortune." Roberta's comment had been wrapped in tones of shock and dismay, no doubt meant to communicate stalwart support of a friend who'd been maligned in the latest rumors circulating, but Marianne strongly questioned the sincerity of the tone. Roberta was not someone Marianne intuitively felt she could trust. It seemed odd that someone who didn't know her well at all would seem inclined to defend her publicly or to share information of a private matter with her as Roberta had done the last time they'd talked.

Marianne's mother was ready to respond to the dubious comment, but Marianne would fight her own battles. She sat up straighter in her chair and fixed her fellow tablemates with a strong stare. "Pennington has been a delightful friend to our family, nothing more. We have a mutual friend in the Countess of Camberly, whom my mother and I had the good opportunity to meet while we were in New York last year."

Roberta made an exaggerated moue. "Then he's not courting you? I had so hoped he was, for your sake, Miss Addison . . ." Her voice, imitating all kindness itself, trailed off.

Mrs. Farnwick patted Roberta's hand. "You are so kind to worry for your friend's well-being." She addressed her next comment to the table at large. "It's refreshing to see girls befriend one another instead of become catty competitors on the marriage mart." Her gaze landed on Marianne. "Still, it's for the best Pennington isn't courting you. News is going around that his finances aren't stable. No real trouble yet, not like Marlborough a few years ago, but concern is starting to rise." She waved her fan. "Marlborough fought the debt as best he could, selling art and his library, even the enamels, before he capitulated and married the American girl."

Marianne heard the multiple meanings embedded in the message: an Englishman worth his merit would sell everything before he'd consider swallowing his pride and marrying an American for her millions. That was the criterion for Alasdair. One should not give in too early to the financial allure of an American wife.

A white-aproned servant brought a tray of tea sweets to the table, saving Marianne from the need to respond. "Ah, lemon scones! Louise's cook has the most delicious recipe I've ever tasted," Mrs. Farnwick gushed, reaching for one of the delicacies as if she'd not slandered the hostess minutes before with the same relish with which she was now eating that hostess' food.

The library of Waltham House was dark and empty, save for the lamp burning low on the carved mantelpiece and the man and the woman conversing in hushed tones. Everyone else was in the ballroom, oblivious to the chicanery being planned down the hall.

"Did you learn anything useful at the tea today?" Lord Brantley began without prelude. Time was of the essence. The last thing he wanted was to be discovered with Roberta Farnwick in a compromising setting.

Who knew who would come through the door in hopes of finding a place for a quick rendezvous?

"She met Pennington through the Countess of Camberly," Roberta said. "Pennington didn't pick her out randomly. He had an introduction." She and Brantley had both originally suspected Pennington had approached her on his own.

"Hmmm. There are too many Americans in London these days," Brantley scoffed. "They're all so busy helping each other to our titles. It's pathetic, really, their attempts to Anglicize themselves."

Roberta smiled sweetly, no doubt trying to remind him that a willing English rose stood right in front of him ready for the plucking as long as a wedding ring went with it. Brantley toyed with a curl lying over Roberta's shoulder and smiled meaningfully at her. He had to give the girl something to string her along. Without Roberta, he'd lose his meager entrée into Marianne Addison's world. He wanted to know what she did, where she went, and what the status of Pennington's intentions were so he could better plan his own strategies.

"How did she meet the countess?" Brantley wondered aloud, going over the earlier comments in his head.

"In New York. Apparently they were there at the same time."

"Hmmm. I don't recall the countess saying anything about the visit, or meeting her prior to Miss

Addison's arriving on our doorstep. Roberta dear, see what you can find out about Miss Addison's trip to New York. Perhaps there's something hiding there we can unearth and use." He dropped the curl, letting it fall against her breast. "You've done well, my dear. Now, go quickly so that you are not noticed. Send me a message when you know anything."

Alone in the room, Brantley stretched out on the long sofa. Miss Addison of San Francisco had been in New York, and yet the countess had not mentioned it except in passing reference. Goodness knew the countess had plenty of opportunities to expand upon that acquaintance. But he sensed that the countess was being deliberately vague in that regard.

Additionally, he'd not been joking when he'd said there were too many Americans in London. Americans had been coming to London for years looking for a title, something to add to their bourgeois collection of things. He'd been in his twenties when the first of them had come, women with daughters who'd not been accepted in New York. San Francisco was a long way from London. It was not a journey one would elect to make without good reason.

What would compel an heiress from the far west to make the trip when surely there were other centers of culture that would do just as nicely and at a shorter distance? Nothing that rivaled London, mind you, but there were numerous elite spas in America, and there was Newport for those who had the access and the money. In fact, many Americans departed London by June, setting aside the zenith of the London Season in lieu of getting to Newport.

Brantley folded his hands behind his head. He smelled a secret. Miss Addison had something to hide, and he was confident in his abilities to ferret out that secret and expose it to the light. Once the secret was out, it would be interesting to see what Pennington would do. Would he walk away from the girl and claim to do his duty by marrying Miss Stewart, or would he attempt to defend the pretty American and justify her secret? It was always interesting, although not always surprising, to see what men would do for money. He would get an inkling of how far Pennington was willing to go tomorrow when he launched his next sally.

Chapter Nine

Alasdair helped himself to a hearty plateful of breakfast from the sideboard in the morning room. He heaped sausage links next to his kippers and eggs. There was nothing like a good breakfast to start off a great day. He was in high spirits. The sun was out for a second day in a row, he was taking Marianne driving in the park later in the afternoon, and she had been a smashing success at the theater. Whatever vindictive recourse Brantley hoped to wreak in accordance with his bet to see her ousted from London by late July looked to be effectively thwarted.

The man could bluster all he wanted. Marianne was taking well, thanks to the efforts of Camberly and Audrey. Alasdair knew that where Audrey led others would follow, especially with Stella heading up the vanguard. Alasdair doubted that Brantley wanted to take on the Camberly prestige once it was firmly established that Marianne had Audrey's sponsorship.

Alasdair set down his plate and took his seat at the empty table, ready to congratulate himself on a hand well played when it came to his strategy with Marianne. Between him and Camberly, they had skillfully managed to buffer her from Brantley's cruel intentions without worrying her over them or calling her attention to Audrey's sponsorship. It had all been neatly negotiated without discussing a thing.

Alasdair forked a sausage and bit deep into it, savoring its spicy juices. Ah, it was a particularly good day.

"What is all this about?" his mother's angry tones demanded from the doorway, giving short warning of her approach. She rattled a newspaper to emphasize her words. A footman efficiently pulled out a chair for her and started to ask about filling a breakfast plate. She dismissed him with an imperious wave of her hand. "Just tea, please." She turned to Alasdair, who was feeling that his particularly good day had just become less so. "I can't eat a bite considering what the papers are writing about you," she scolded.

Alasdair set down his fork, giving his mother all his attention. "What are they writing, may I ask?"

She shoved the page under his nose. "More tripe about you and the American girl. This columnist seems very informed about your whereabouts: you sat with that American at the Radcliffe musicale, and you escorted her to the theater. You have been officially and publicly linked to her. Perhaps we could discard the first mention in the papers as nothing more than social speculation. But now, to have it done a second time! Everyone will assume you have serious intentions toward her. You should have known better, Alasdair. This article even mentions poor Sarah again and your previous understanding with her."

Alasdair bore her tirade stoically. In the end, she could rant all she wanted and he would do what he preferred, he reminded himself.

"It's absolutely scandalous to be the focus of so much attention," his mother huffed.

Alasdair read through the article, tuning out his mother's plans. The article was alarming to him, but not for the reasons his mother itemized. The article wasn't so much about him as about Marianne—what she wore, where she'd gone even without him. There was mention of a comment she'd made at Mrs. Mackay's tea that suggested she might be mocking the English way of things, and certainly illustrated her tendency toward free speaking.

It occurred to Alasdair that Brantley likely had a hand in directing the columnist's ideas and information. Alasdair knew it was not uncommon for the financially pressed among his circles to discreetly sell information about exclusive events to society pages in order to make some pocket change. Nor was it beyond

the pale, for those who could afford it, to pay a writer
to mention them in the column or link them to prestigious people.

But what disturbed him most was that Brantley had
someone helping him, likely a woman who would be
at primarily female events like Mrs. Mackay's tea.
Such organization and planned malice affirmed the
level of wickedness to which Brantley would stoop
without a qualm.

Fighting his battle in the press gave Brantley an advantage as well as protection. He could hide behind
the columnist's words. He was invisible while his
words were read by everyone, and thus did not have
to be accountable for his prejudice.

"I think we should announce your engagement
to Sarah Stewart immediately. That will set things to
rights. We can have an announcement made in the
Times," his mother proclaimed loudly.

"No," Alasdair said staunchly in a knee-jerk response. He'd been saying "no" for so long about the
Sarah Stewart situation that he responded on reflex.
He rose, leaving his plate of eggs and kippers mostly
untouched. The only way to win an argument with his
mother was simply to leave the room. "Please, excuse
me. I have work to see to."

Two hours later, Alasdair raked his hands through
his thick dark hair, ruffling it in frustration. His solicitor sat patiently across from him in the room that

served as Alasdair's office at the town house. The session hadn't gone as well as Alasdair had hoped it would. He'd planned the budget for the Season meticulously, down to the last pound. The country estate was running with a skeleton staff and all the extra wings of the house were closed so that the house could function at maximum efficiency with minimal output. Now, a note from the prince strongly hinted at his desire to have a house party there.

Alasdair groaned at the prospect. House parties were inherently expensive regardless of who was invited. But hosting the prince was exorbitant. For starters, he'd have to close the Richmond house where his mother preferred to stay, coming into Town only on occasion for special events, for the remainder of the Season. Frankly, Alasdair preferred she stay there too. They got along best at a distance. Now she would be in his pockets for the rest of the Season, sharing the town house. But there was no question of affording the Richmond house and the London town house with Bertie coming for a week. Of course, his mother would understand. She always understood when it came to his friendship with Bertie. One could not refuse the prince without sacrificing the prince's favor, and his mother was very fond of his status in the prince's circle of friends. The prince was currently away at Brighton, and so far Alasdair had avoided extra extravagances in Town due to his absence.

"We'd best start with a list," Alasdair instructed his solicitor. A list didn't begin to cover it. There would be new linens to purchase, rooms to restore, and gardens to tend just to get ready. Then there were the guest lists to assemble and the menus to plan. The prince had an expensive penchant for lobster salad and other delicacies including Charles Heidsieck's champagne. He'd need help. Perhaps Audrey and Stella could assist. One good piece of news about the house party was that he could use it to introduce Marianne to the prince. Brantley would never dare to cross Bertie.

After giving instructions and the rudimentary elements of a list to his solicitor, Alasdair decided it was time for a walk. He needed to talk with Camberly, and he had a visit to pay a particular journalist at the *Morning Post* who would soon be writing a lot less about him and Marianne Addison.

Alasdair immediately forgot his troubles when he sighted Marianne in the town house garden on Portland Square that afternoon. He was used to finding her in the garden now. She sat on a low bench near the fountain, engaged in a book and entirely unaware of his presence. He stood silently for a moment, taking in her unrestrained beauty. She was dressed in a pale-nougat-and-pink-striped carriage gown for their drive. The soft palette of colors evoked the mood of an innocent summer day and set off her ivory complexion and golden curls—an intoxicating combination to be sure. He appreciated that there was no artifice about her loveliness. She was simply herself.

Alasdair walked stealthily up behind her, careful not to let the gravel of the path crunch beneath his feet. No one was around, so he slipped his hands over her eyes. "Guess who."

Marianne laughed. "I can smell lavender and sage. It must be Alasdair."

"You can smell me?" Alasdair removed his hands and stepped back, intrigued by her comment. "I don't think anyone has ever 'smelled' me before." Indeed, he couldn't think of a single woman he'd ever been involved with who had mentioned smelling him.

"Well, it's such a lovely smell, all that sage and lavender—I can't imagine how anyone could overlook it," Marianne said in her own defense.

"Don't forget the artemisia," Alasdair teased.

"Artemisia, of course." Marianne smiled. "I knew I smelled something else. But it's been keeping me guessing." She stood up and closed her book. "Are we ready to go? I've been looking forward to this all day."

Alasdair hoped the drive lived up to her expectations. He worried about the reactions of others now that the second article had been published. In an attempt to avoid exposing Marianne to any hostility, he'd arranged for Camberly and Lionel to join them in the park, and he had hopes that with the buffer of her friends about her, Marianne wouldn't notice the difference. It was starting to cross Alasdair's mind that he would have to explain everything to her very soon.

Marianne waited until they'd strolled a slight distance away from Camberly and Lionel and their wives to bring up the tender subject. "Do you mind explaining what is going on?" she asked quietly once they were out of earshot.

"Going on?" Alasdair answered vaguely, hoping to play the obtuse fellow.

"What's Camberly doing here? People seemed different today, less friendly in their greetings. Does it have to do with the article? I saw that we were mentioned in the social column again, and I assume it is distressing for you. I apologize for having caused any trouble, but I didn't think about the implications of my comment at the tea. I never dreamed it would end up in a newspaper for the world to see."

Alasdair shook his head. "No, you've not caused any trouble." He took her hand and pulled her behind a tree. Her blue eyes were earnest and concerned. He couldn't bear for her to think that she'd failed him in some way.

He had not meant to tell her, here in the middle of the park, but the words came tumbling out. "I am afraid my spilling of the champagne wasn't such a brilliant idea after all. I underestimated how much Brantley wanted to dance with you and I fear I've put you in the middle of his plans to bring me down a peg.

"He's made himself your enemy, Marianne, all in

an attempt to get back at me. There's a wager he's placed in the betting book at White's. He and another of his cronies, Hamsford, have bet how long you'll last in London before you're ousted."

Marianne's smile faded. Her glance fell to her feet. "I've made it fairly easy for him with my remark at the tea. How long have you known?" She brought her gaze back up, peering at him from beneath the wide brim of her hat.

"Since the Radcliffe musicale."

He watched Marianne's mind working through the events of the past weeks. "I see," she said a quietly. "I never suspected a thing. You were quite clever, insinuating me into your group of friends, lending me their protection without actually telling me, letting me believe they were my friends too."

Alasdair sucked in a deep breath. He'd not thought of his actions from that point of view. He'd never once wanted her to feel betrayed or manipulated, but in trying to avoid those circumstances he'd caused them to occur anyway. "Camberly and Audrey, Lionel and Stella, all like you. They respect you. Their friendship is genuine," Alasdair argued, wanting to alleviate the hurt and the doubt in her eyes.

"Very well," Marianne said, but in a tone that indicated she didn't quite believe him.

They were out of other people's view. Alasdair reached for her hand. "I did not mean for any of this to hurt you. I went to the journalist's workplace today and asked him not to write about us in quite so much detail. I hope I succeeded in being more persuasive than Brantley was."

"Brantley?"

"I am sure he's the one giving the information to the journalists, although I'm not sure where he's getting it. If he stops, the negative press should stop," Alasdair reasoned. His mouth quirked up into a smile. "Of course, I told the journalist I wasn't opposed to him writing about *me*, only about the lurid, unsubstantiated *analysis* that tends to accompany the reports."

Alasdair had to give Marianne credit. She was taking the news well; she could have been far more dismayed. "I do have good news too," Alasdair said, turning the conversation away from Brantley's attempt to instigate a scandal. "The prince is coming to a house party at my estate before Cowes. It will be a fabulous time for you to meet him."

Marianne was suitably impressed enough to make him believe the cost would be worth it just to see her smile.

He wanted to kiss that smile. He'd thought of little else when he had the choice; the memory of that one quick kiss in the rowboat had lingered powerfully. Alasdair leaned in, hands resting on either side of the tree trunk, framing her lovely face. He bent his lips to hers, finding them already parted, already anticipating his kiss. This was the hard part, Alasdair thought. She was eager and beautiful, and she understood him even if she didn't know him yet. She might not know his favorite color or how he took his tea, but she understood the things that drove him. Their conversation at the Tower had proved as much. He could propose and put his money worries to rest forever, but to do that so soon would make him the very villain the papers were making him out to be. Marianne deserved a legitimate courtship, a real chance to decide if he was right for her. Besides, he would not give Brantley the satisfaction of painting him with the fortune-hunter's brush.

Brantley lifted the note, placed facedown on a salver so that no one could see the address or direction of the sender. He smiled while he read it. The note wasn't from Roberta, as he'd suspected it would be. It was from the journalist he'd paid to draw attention to the unsavory undertones of Pennington's association with Miss Addison. The journalist was nervous. Pennington had paid him a visit that included a bloody nose.

Such behavior was telling. Pennington must have developed quite a tendre for the pretty American to risk a ruckus. Pennington's fist might have stopped the machine of British media, Brantley mused, but it couldn't squelch the scandal altogether. Word of mouth among the ton could be just as deadly as the printed word, especially with the juicy tidbit Miss Farnwick had delivered to him earlier that afternoon: Miss Addison had been given the cut direct in New York for attending a Champagne Sunday. It was too delicious to idly let it drop in casual conversation. He would wait and watch for the right moment when its effect could be most devastating.

Brantley had no concerns about how devastating it would be. It would be shattering to Pennington, who'd already demonstrated that he'd opt to try and protect Miss Addison, no doubt believing she was innocent in the ways of social intrigues. Pennington would be crushed by the news that his trust in Miss Addison's virtue was misplaced. No man liked to feel that his more-chivalrous sentiments were betrayed. But first, Brantley thought, there might be some financial gains to be made with this latest bit of leverage.

Chapter Ten

Alasdair checked his watch yet another time. Three o'clock. His friends and Marianne should be arriving at any time. He'd been thinking that since noon. He paced the length of his study, too impatient to work. He'd come down early in the week with his mother to oversee the general readiness for the house party, and he'd missed Marianne terribly, far more than he'd anticipated.

He was tempted to ride out and see if he could meet the carriages but that would only add fuel to his mother's growing resentment toward Marianne. They'd fought twice, in regard to his affections for Marianne, within the past seven days—once at dinner the first night, and then later when he'd informed his mother that he'd called on Sarah Stewart and told her in no uncertain terms that there would not be a proposal from him.

It had been a difficult week. There had been the house to prepare, and wings to open, and there'd been relationships to prepare as well. Alasdair wanted everything perfect for Marianne as much as he wanted everything ready for his friend the prince. He'd felt it was important that he clear up his situation with Sarah before Marianne arrived.

The conversation with Sarah had gone well. He had discussed nullifying the arrangement with her. She was not surprised, and even seemed a bit relieved that at last she could put an end to the waiting and wondering. He'd also told her about Marianne. It was an unlooked-for boon that Sarah had become the one person he could talk to about Marianne that week. Alasdair knew he could count on her to help buffer Marianne from his mother's acerbic comments.

All that remained was for Marianne to arrive. Alasdair idly fiddled with an inkwell on the wide cherry-wood desk. As much as he missed her, as much as he'd waited all week for her to join him at Highborough, the family seat, he was anxious now that the hour of her arrival was drawing near. What would she think of Highborough? Would she think, as he did, that Highborough was an empty tomb of a house, all cold stone and high walls?

Alasdair detested the family seat. All of its elegance, all of its portraits and expensive collections could not bring warmth to its cavernous halls. A family would do all that—a real family with children who yelled and ran through the house flying kites, who tried to slide down bannisters and filch biscuits from the kitchens.

Alasdair sighed. The potential had always been there to make Highborough something more than it was. Would Marianne see it? Or would she see a majestic house, a showplace, that was starting to age, its expensive carpets starting to fade and fray after generations, its furniture having a slightly careworn quality to its upholstery, and its roof tending to leak during a heavy rain? He very much feared she'd take one look at Highborough and see a house that needed her fortune to maintain itself.

That wasn't what he wanted her to see. He wanted her to see the potential for something more. He wanted her to share his dream of putting a lively family in these halls and making it a true home. He'd waited a long time for a woman who could share that dream. He thought he'd found that woman in Marianne. Alasdair flipped open his watch again and stared ruefully at the time. They should have been here by now.

Four carriages made a grand procession down the Devonshire country road that led to the parklands preceding the Pennington family seat. It had taken four days to make the journey from London to the Pennington estate. Good weather and the general merriment of the group had broken up the tedium of travel. The carriages often stopped at sights of interest to show off the striking landscape for Marianne's benefit. The afternoons were marked by picnics that allowed the travelers a chance to walk and stretch their legs. The journey could have been accomplished in three days, but the group had chosen to enjoy the travel rather than to make a misery of it.

For her part, Marianne was glad for the respite. In the weeks since the papers had mentioned her outspoken remark at Mrs. Mackay's tea, no further issues had cropped up. Brantley's threats seemed to have been effectively managed by Alasdair's visit to the unfortunate journalist, although there had been a bit of a stir once others got wind of the story.

The stir-up hadn't lasted long. Another bit of gossip about a girl who had eloped quickly took precedent. Marianne was more than happy to relinquish the spotlight to another unfortunate. As a result, the weeks had been filled with nothing but the social whir of the Season. Even Roberta Farnwick had stepped to the fringes of her social circle, which made the busyness of the Season much more palatable; Marianne was certain she had Audrey to thank for that. Roberta Farnwick and her mother did not dare to move in the exalted circles frequented by Camberly and Pennington.

The only item that would have made the last few weeks more enjoyable would have been a chance to see more of Alasdair. By no means had he abandoned her, but the ensuing house party for the prince had taken up a considerable amount of his time. He'd left Town last week to see to the final preparations.

Marianne was eager to see him again. Although Audrey and Stella had kept her too busy to dwell on Alasdair's absence, the parties and routs had seemed duller without Alasdair's quick wit and easy smile beside her.

Her eagerness to see Alasdair competed with her nerves over attending her first-ever house party. The prince would be there. So would Alasdair's mother and, Marianne assumed, the woman Alasdair was expected to marry, Sarah Stewart. No one had said as much to her. Marianne expected Audrey and Stella were trying to be polite in omitting such a reference. But it only made sense that the woman would be there. She was a neighbor, after all, and a longtime family friend. Marianne thought it would be the worst type of snub to simply ignore her and not extend an invitation. Alasdair would not be small-minded enough to behave in such a manner.

The carriage rounded a corner and Audrey leaned toward her, excitement in her voice. "Alasdair's home is beautiful. You should be able to see it come into view any moment now. There it is. Do you see it through the trees?"

Marianne adjusted her seat for a better view. "Oh," she gasped. Even the little bit she could glimpse was astounding. By the time the whole house came into view, she was mesmerized.

The Georgian facade of the house stretched into two

long wings flanking the marble-columned entrance and the curved stairs leading from the drive to the enormous front door. The driveway ended in a loop so that carriages could drop off passengers and head toward the stables without needing to back up. The center of that loop was graced with a mini-version of a meticulously kept Alpine garden complete with mountain rocks strategically placed among the profusion of white and violet wildflowers and spindly pine.

"The house is spectacular," Marianne whispered in awe. Alasdair had once referred to his home as the "old pile." From his reference, she'd envisioned something of a more ramshackle nature. "I can see why the prince wanted to come here. I'd never leave this place."

Audrey laughed and leaned forward to impart a confidence. "I agree, but the English will tell you that life in the countryside is too dull for them."

Their carriage pulled to a halt behind the one carrying Lionel and Stella. Camberly jumped down and helped Marianne and Audrey out. The third carriage, carrying her parents, pulled up behind them. By the time they'd reached the top of the stairs, Alasdair was there to meet them. Marianne hung back, letting Lionel and Camberly greet their friend.

She had not seen Alasdair in over a week, and now, watching him with his friends in his own personal venue, she felt like she was seeing him for the first time. Certainly he was still the same handsome, dark-haired, dark-eyed man with the broad shoulders she loved to hold while dancing; physically, he looked the same as always. But there was an undeniable change. In London, Marianne had often forgotten he was the Viscount Pennington. There, it had been easy to think of him as merely a gentleman. Now, she could see it more clearly. Here, in the countryside, at his family seat, the mantle of being the viscount sat squarely and almost tangibly upon those broad shoulders of his.

Marianne was struck at once by the reservation in his manner, the stiff formality he exuded even when greeting his friends. She'd thought that, once in the country, away from the standards of the ton, he'd be even more relaxed than he usually appeared. She could see immediately that she was wrong about that.

The little group parted and Alasdair strode toward her. "Miss Addison, welcome to Highborough, family seat to four generations of Penningtons." He bowed over her hand and greeted her parents with the same polite enthusiasm. This was not the sort of reunion she'd imagined. A frightening thought swept her: Had Alasdair changed his mind? Had he come home and imagined her in this elegant, traditional setting and failed to see her fitting in? Worse, had he come home and seen Sarah Stewart? Perhaps, in that case, absence had made the heart grow fonder.

These thoughts plagued her to distraction as she oversaw the unpacking of her trunk. By the time the dinner hour neared, Marianne's apprehensions were mounting. No matter how often she told herself that it was ridiculous to let her speculations unnerve her, the butterflies in her stomach continued to flutter. She was thankful that they'd all been able to arrive in advance of the other guests. The rest of the party guests wouldn't arrive for another four days, giving Stella and Audrey time to help Alasdair with last-minute preparations.

There was a knock on her door and Marianne was glad to see her mother there, instead of one of the many maids who'd been parading in and out of her chambers, whisking dresses off to be pressed. There seemed to be an enormous amount of maids assigned singly to see to her needs.

"You seem relieved to see me." Her mother offered a gentle smile, sitting down on the corner of Marianne's bed. She was already dressed for dinner in a tasteful gown of dark blue silk trimmed in cream lace. She looked elegant and confident. Marianne wished she could feel at least half that collected.

"I am," Marianne confessed. She pulled the small white chair from the dressing table near the bed. "There are so many people to help me with everything imaginable. It's quite overwhelming. I am perfectly capable of brushing my own hair and picking out my own dresses."

Elizabeth Addison laughed softly. "England is a different world, isn't it? Is it all you'd hoped?"

"It's more than I'd hoped," Marianne replied, realizing the truth of it for the first time. "I never anticipated lifestyles on this grand scale or the opportunity to meet the prince. I had no idea the size of estates was so large." She'd planned carefully before their departure from San Francisco. There had been the appointments with Worth, the tutoring from a reputable Englishwoman living in Paris about the mind-boggling assortment of appropriate forms of address, and a crash course in English life and culture. But none of it met up with the realities of seeing the English peerage in action up close. Marianne had planned her campaign with immense attention to detail and still it hadn't been enough.

Her mother reached for her hand to squeeze in reassurance. "I think you're doing very well. We all are. Your father has made some good business contacts through Camberly and Lionel. He's looking forward to the racing at Cowes immensely. And I've enjoyed seeing a different part of the world, despite how overwhelming it can be at times."

"Doing well?" Marianne countered. "I'm unsure of that. I've teetered on the brink of scandal since my arrival."

"I'm not convinced it is so much the brink of scandal as it is a natural consequence of popularity, Marianne. You didn't ask to be the center of attention, but it happened anyway." Marianne had confided all of Alasdair's details to her mother. Elizabeth was well aware of Brantley's shenanigans. But to her credit, she'd brushed it aside.

"Besides, Marianne, we know you've done nothing

wrong. The English have a decidedly different outlook on what constitutes a scandal than we do. In fact, they have quite a different outlook on many things. I think they like to see our fortunes and conveniently forget how they were acquired, even if it was through honest hard work."

She paused and then added, "Your father and I laugh over the improbability of our situation. It's a fabulous dream to think that a baker's son and his wife, the daughter of a New England college professor, are dining among the aristocracy, soon to meet the future king of England."

Marianne smiled at that. Theirs was indeed quite an American tale, made of the stuff of dreams. Then her smile faded. Would Alasdair laugh at such fantasy? He'd been raised to dine with dukes and monarchs his entire life. What could he possibly want with a baker's granddaughter?

"You're thinking about the viscount," her mother divined. "Do you like him?"

Marianne gave a nervous laugh. "I've enjoyed his company very much in London. But here, he appears different. Today on the steps, I felt that I was meeting him for the first time and I realized exactly how dissimilar our backgrounds are."

"It must be a grave undertaking to host the prince, my dear. The viscount is no doubt under a large strain."

"What if he's decided that he likes Sarah Stewart better than me?" Marianne blurted out.

"Then you'll both be infinitely happier in the long run, my dear." Elizabeth smiled. "You could never be happy with a man who thought he loved another. You deserve better than that." She paused, assessing Marianne with a gaze that made her daughter fidget. Marianne loved her mother, but sometimes she saw too much. "I know you came here motivated in large part by what happened in New York," said her mother. "I think it was the right decision to come to London. If you fall off a horse, you have to get right back up. Maybe, you even thought to grab yourself a title. However, I don't think you thought about everything attendant with accomplishing that goal, such as the husband that would go with the title."

Marianne gave a wry smile of admission. It sounded a bit on the petty side when her mother explained it like that, but at least her mother understood her initial motivations and understood that something stronger than pettiness had motivated her actions. She'd wanted more than girlish revenge when she'd set out on this path. She'd wanted redemption, and perhaps even a type of justice for the cruel prank that had been pulled on her with such severe repercussions.

"Have you and Alasdair reached any kind of understanding I should know about?" Elizabeth inquired politely, rising from the bed to search through Marianne's wardrobe.

Although Marianne had shared Brantley's schemes with her mother, she had not shared all the details of her association with Alasdair. For all that her mother had seen from the outside looking in was a man who'd escorted Marianne to several social functions as part of a group. He'd always acted with decorum. His behavior, while befitting a suitor, was also the impeccable behavior of a polite family friend wishing only to include Marianne and her family in his circle of acquaintances. Truly, if the newspapers hadn't lent a torrid edge to their association, no one would have thought Alasdair's interest was motivated by anything other than politeness. Marianne herself might have believed it too if it hadn't been for those two kisses.

Marianne blushed. "He said in London that he wished to court me. He said we deserved a chance to see if we suited one another."

Her mother nodded approvingly. "He's a smart man, then, who knows the value of a good marriage and that the value isn't necessarily calculated in financial wealth."

"Perhaps. Maybe he wants to see if I fit, if I can be a countess," Marianne remarked ruefully.

Her mother turned from her perusal of the wardrobe, a warning in her tone. "You do not have to remake yourself for any man, Marianne. You can be a countess, perhaps just a different type of countess than what they're used to seeing over here. Audrey St. Clair-Maddox has done an admirable job from what I can tell. Of course, I don't know her all that well, but she seems well adjusted. More importantly, she seems happy, as does Camberly—although I doubt she's the countess he thought he'd have. She runs a music school for girls and continues her own career as a pianist."

Marianne nodded. She understood what her mother was saying and it made sense to keep herself intact. A man who wanted the outer shell of who she was, but who didn't want the inner layers that went with it—all her opinions and beliefs—was not a man to be desired. But it wasn't that simple in reality. She was falling in love with Alasdair Braden and she desperately wanted him to love her in return.

"How about the ivory gown?" Her mother held up a dress exquisitely embroidered around the hem with seed pearls. It was one of Marianne's favorites for its simple yet graceful design. But tonight she wanted to stand out, to remind Alasdair that she was in the room no matter who else was there. Marianne shook her head. "I had thought to wear the royal blue silk."

Her mother nodded sagely. "Save it for the house party. The ivory gown will accomplish what you wish."

In the end, Marianne knew her mother was right. She surveyed the effect of the gown in the long looking glass in her room. Worth's gifted tailoring fit the gown perfectly to the trim line of her waist and emphasized her long legs with the sweep of the skirt that swished softly as she walked. The bodice showed off the feminine slope of her shoulders. The wrap Worth had created from antique lace, to go especially with the gown,

completed the ensemble perfectly. Marianne was glad
now to have bowed to his finer judgment in that regard.
She'd secretly thought the lace wrap no more than a
scrap of material to be toted around. Now, as she saw
the final image, she was happy to have kept that
thought to herself.

The woman who wore this gown was more than a
debutante in a standard pale-colored dress. This woman
was loveliness itself, existing in that precarious bal-
ance between naive innocence and worldliness. In any
case, neither of those attributes suited Marianne. No
one growing up in San Francisco as she'd done could
ever compete with the total ingenuousness of the English schoolroom miss who'd seen nothing of life; neither could she claim, although well educated, to be a
scholar of the world and its many vices. Which was as
it should be.

Marianne's confidence was restored as she followed
her parents down to the drawing room to meet the others for dinner. Audrey greeted them warmly, drawing
them into the conversation with effortless skill, while
Camberly inquired about the latest update on her father's yacht.

From the corner of her eye, Marianne spotted Alasdair by the long window talking with an older gentleman. He said something to the man and began making
his way toward her, the smile she had enjoyed so much
in London on his lips. Perhaps it had been the strain of

the party, after all, that had caused him to look so stern earlier. He seemed perfectly fine now. Marianne couldn't help but smile back, so great was her relief.

"You look beautiful," he said, bowing over her gloved hand. "I've come to steal her away, Lady Camberly," he said to Audrey, catching Marianne by surprise. Whenever Alasdair had been *en famille* with his close friends, he'd always called Lady Camberly "Audrey." Marianne had to think for a moment about who he was referring to, so foreign was the reference.

"Come, there are people I want you to meet," Alasdair said, taking Marianne by the elbow. He guided her to where the man still stood at the window, looking out over the vast parkland of the estate.

"Mr. Stewart, I would like for you to meet Miss Marianne Addison of San Francisco," Alasdair began formally. He turned slightly and Marianne noticed for the first time that someone else was sitting in the chair by the long curtains that framed the window. The woman in the chair was youngish, in her midtwenties, and might have been passably attractive if she hadn't worn a gown that blended so ideally with the deep forest green of the draperies. The gown contained almost nothing in the way of trimmings that might have set it apart from the curtains. Her brown hair was styled in a simple chignon that was held in a net, and her very demeanor was quiet and withdrawn, making it easy to overlook her presence. Marianne knew who this woman was before Alasdair told her, but it still came as a shock to hear the words come his lips. "Miss Addison, I'd also like to introduce his daughter, Miss Sarah Stewart."

Marianne greeted Sarah Stewart in as polite and as friendly a manner as she could. All the while, her thoughts ran riot. This was the woman his mother wanted him to marry? Marianne couldn't imagine a more unlikely pairing. Did the woman not know her son at all? Alasdair was a vibrant man, full of life and energy. The woman in the chair was an expert at making herself invisible.

Miss Stewart smiled and said warmly, "So this is the girl you've talked about so much, Pennington." She turned back to Marianne. "I am so pleased to meet you, Miss Addison. He's talked of nothing but you since he arrived last week and now I can see why. You're here at last, and we can be friends." She rose from her chair and looped her arm through Marianne's. "I want to hear all about San Francisco. I would love to travel, myself, but my responsibilities don't permit me to go very far for very long."

"She's a good girl, my Sarah is," Mr. Stewart said with gruff affection. "She knows her father can't get on without her. She runs my house with an efficiency I can't match."

"Come stroll with me. We have at least fifteen minutes before the dinner bell sounds. You can tell me about the hills and how the trolley cars manage on them."

Marianne had not expected to like Sarah Stewart, but as they talked she found it nearly impossible not to like the young woman whose interest seemed sincere and entirely unlike the superficial friendliness offered by Roberta Farnwick. Their conversation was progressing well when Alasdair joined them, an older woman on his arm.

"Miss Addison, I am sorry to interrupt, but there's another introduction I'd like to make. Miss Addison, I'd like for you to meet my mother, the dowager countess Pennington."

Chapter Eleven

Marianne could tell immediately that this was not going to turn out to be a pleasant surprise as meeting Miss Stewart had been. Alasdair's mother glared at her with a narrow gaze, effectively communicating precisely what the woman thought of her: that she was an American nobody far beneath her notice and certainly too far beneath her son to warrant the attentions he paid her.

Marianne greeted her with all the respect due the woman's station, a bit shocked at the woman's openly intense dislike. She'd been prepared to meet a woman who tried to meddle in her grown son's life, but she hadn't been prepared for the extreme loathing the woman displayed. Marianne tried to ignore Lady Pennington's behavior. "Your son has been the most

141

dedicated of escorts in London. He's gone out of his way to see to our comfort."

"Quite so." The woman returned with a supercilious coldness. Sarah, standing next to her, blushed and Alasdair's jaw tightened, as though both were mortified by the countess' poor manners.

In her peripheral vision, Marianne caught a glimpse of her father talking with his usual enthusiasm to a group gathered about him as all nodded their heads. Seeing him reminded her of something he'd once said. She understood perfectly now. Alasdair's mother didn't detest her as much as the woman feared her. Her father had once told her that people often hated whatever threatened them. Hatred followed closely on the heels of fear. For whatever reason, Alasdair's mother feared her.

The notion of this formidable dowager fearing a young woman from San Francisco struck Marianne as oddly hilarious, not to mention ridiculous. Marianne couldn't imagine any reason for the woman to feel threatened by her. Nonetheless, she did.

The group was saved from any further need to converse by the announcement for dinner, which brought Camberly over to the group, bowing suavely to Alasdair's mother, ready to take her into dinner.

"Ladies, please excuse me," Alasdair made a quick nod and departed. It took Marianne a moment to realize why he'd left them. She'd initially thought it odd when there were two ladies waiting to go into dinner standing right there with him. Then she remembered the importance the English put on the seating precedence. Of course, Alasdair was off to escort Audrey into dinner as the next-highest-ranking woman in the room, followed by Stella giving her arm to Sarah's father, and Lionel coming over to escort Sarah.

As the line began to form, it became obvious that there was an odd number of men. As the lowest-ranking female in the room, Marianne would be left out. She refused to let it upset her and prepared to take her father's other arm when she saw Audrey whisper something to Alasdair, causing him to smile. He left Audrey and strode to Marianne's side. "Miss Addison, please join us" was all he said, but Marianne saw a twinkle in his eye that suggested he was quite pleased about thwarting his mother's subtle intentions.

Marianne gave him a brave smile and gladly took his arm while he rejoined Audrey, second in line. The three of them went in to dinner together.

But Alasdair's mother wasn't bested yet. Once soup was served, she asked, "How does dinner seating in America compare to seating here?"

Marianne opted for the high road and replied sweetly, "The guest of honor sits at the host's right hand, Lady Pennington. Other than that, for the most part, we sit where we'd like, within reason of course."

Lady Pennington looked ready to sniff in disdain at the anarchy Marianne had suggested. Marianne was willing to let the woman's implied insult rest but

Audrey wasn't. "For more formal occasions we decide seating precedent based on money. The richest people at the table sit above the salt and the poorer sit below. Of course, that's all quite relative since Wall Street fortunes fluctuate on regular occasion."

Marianne took a sip of wine from her glass to cover her amusement. Lady Pennington looked aghast at Audrey's casual comment about money. It was clear that having such public knowledge of such an intimate subject was positively abhorrent.

Audrey wasn't finished. "It's much simpler, and frankly, it makes more sense. The rules here are positively ridiculous. A husband and wife are less likely to walk into together than a father and his daughter. No young girl relishes the idea of walking with her father when there's a handsome eligible peer in the room. Why, it's a matchmaking opportunity gone to waste." Audrey reached for her glass and eyed the other guests, waiting for their reaction.

"Here, here," Lionel tapped on his crystal goblet with a spoon. "There are nearly as many Americans at this table as there are Brits," he said, making it clear that Lady Pennington had managed to insult not just Marianne, but half of the other dinner guests as well. "In honor of the five of us at the table, I propose a toast to America and its simplicity. May it never be so difficult to sit down to table as it is in England."

Everyone laughed, most of them good-naturedly. Lady Pennington participated only grudgingly. With admirable skill, Sarah Stewart picked up the conversation after the toast, leading the discussion into travels and faraway places.

Alasdair was immeasurably grateful for Lionel's toast. The rest of dinner progressed smoothly. The Stewarts were pleasant dinner guests and responded with interest to the stories Marianne's father told about the baking industry in San Francisco. The others knew each other and conversation flowed easily. He would have enjoyed the meal completely if it hadn't been for his mother's dark mood at the foot of the table, hovering around the meal like a threatening shadow. Her behavior had been purposely rude to Marianne and he would not tolerate it. He'd itched to defend Marianne when his mother had all but cut her dead upon introduction. Her perfunctory words, "Quite so," had been worse than a direct snubbing.

But Marianne had been more than up to the task of coping with his mother. Alasdair had been pleased to see Marianne make the most of the awkward introduction. In fact, he'd been pleased with her all night, although he doubted anything about her could be disappointing. She'd traveled to a home she'd never seen, met people she didn't know except through reputation, knowing that everything she did or said would be looked upon askance and with suspicion simply because she wasn't English. Worse than not being English, she was the competition.

Alasdair watched with regret as the women departed the dining room. He didn't want to imagine what his mother might say or imply in the privacy of the drawing room, out from under his watchful eye. But Marianne was surrounded by friends. Even Sarah had graciously offered her friendship. Audrey would not let his mother run roughshod over Marianne. Audrey would step in if needed, although Marianne was more than capable of fighting her own battles with her own resourceful wit and insight.

Thankfully, the men decided to cut short the masculine pleasure of cigars and brandy after dinner and rejoined the women in the drawing room after only twenty minutes. The scene that met Alasdair's eyes was placid enough to suit him, his eye immediately going to Marianne who sat with Sarah at one cluster of chairs looking at slides through a stereoscope. At a larger cluster containing a gold-and-white-striped sofa, his mother sat with Audrey, Stella, and Elizabeth Addison.

Audrey rose upon seeing the men enter and took charge of the evening's quiet activities. With quick efficiency, she divided the group up for cards, conveniently leaving Alasdair and Marianne on their own. Alasdair could not have orchestrated such a feat if he'd tried. He shot Audrey a thankful grin.

"Miss Addison would probably enjoy a tour of the gardens, Pennington," Audrey said, sitting down to cards across from Camberly. "The gardens are lovely in the evening with their lights on, Miss Addison. Pennington has arranged the most unique situation for showing off his gardens, very modern."

Alasdair watched Marianne stifle a smile at the formality of Audrey's comment. The cheeky girl was laughing at them. Well, he couldn't blame her. It did seem unnecessarily stiff to be addressing everyone formally when everyone here knew each other far better than that. But, for his mother's sake, they tolerated the tradition.

He offered Marianne his arm, hardly able to wait until they were out of earshot to speak with her, really speak with her. He had not spoken with her for over a week and all he'd been able to do since her arrival was treat her as he would any other guest, when all he truly wanted to do was sweep her into his arms and declare to the world that she was his. But such an action would invoke all the scandal he'd tried so hard to avoid.

Her hand trembled slightly on his sleeve. Ah, she felt it too, the need to escape the suffocating formality of the evening. He would give anything to simply be Alasdair and Marianne, to laugh with her without worrying who heard, to kiss her without worrying over who might see them.

Alasdair turned the handle of the French doors leading out onto the wide terrace, letting the evening air cool his heated body. "We can breathe out here." Alasdair turned to Marianne, grateful to be alone with her at last, although he was well aware that they were highly visible yet to those inside the drawing room. Still, no one could hear them, and that was the best privacy he was going to get.

"This is beautiful." Marianne's gaze was focused on the gardens that spread beyond the terrace. "You've lit the gardens with gaslights. How clever. It's a wonder everyone isn't doing it." Every several yards, tall wrought-iron posts rose along the gravel walkways bearing a lantern with a gaslight, illuminating the path so that the garden could be appreciated in the evening.

"The idea came to me when I was in London a couple years ago. I was admiring the street lamps and I thought: Why not transport that idea to my gardens?" Alasdair explained.

"So, you're an inventor of sorts," Marianne said, sounding impressed as she turned her attention from the gardens to him, making him the focus of her blue gaze. The mental pictures of her that he'd carried throughout the week had not done her justice. Her eyes were bluer, her hair a brighter gold than he recalled.

" 'Inventor' is a bit strong of a word. I didn't create anything. I only applied an idea to a new setting." He liked that she appreciated his efforts. "I confess that I enjoy the new inventions this modern age brings us. I appreciate wholeheartedly that I am lucky enough to live in an age of accessible wonder." He'd never spoken such sentiments publicly before. Most of his peers had very little appreciation for the advancements being born around them.

Marianne smiled. "I like to think of this as an era of efficiency. We're able to travel so much farther in a much quicker manner. To think it only took two weeks to cross the Atlantic when it used to take months. And we did it in luxury. We had every comfort aboard ship. My father's bakery was one of the first businesses in San Francisco to deliver bread to people's homes by delivery wagon so that they didn't have to walk to the bakery. This way, there's fresh bread on the table every morning." She paused suddenly, her eyes searching his face.

"What is it?" Alasdair asked, unsure what had caused her look of concern.

"I shouldn't talk of my father's business. I am sure it is far too plebian for your tastes."

"Hardly. I meant it when I said I admire all the new inventions around us and I admire people like your father. Men like him are the new pioneers, the new aristocracy."

"Not everyone likes newness or change," Marianne observed.

"No, not everyone." He knew she was thinking about his mother.

"Your mother doesn't. She doesn't like me. My money is too new." Marianne cut to the point, her eyes fixing him with a stare that demanded full honesty from him.

"I'd be foolish to deny that," Alasdair replied, reaching for one of Marianne's hands. He couldn't bear to be this close to her and not touch her. He placed a light kiss on her knuckles. "But I like you. I like you very much, as I have mentioned on more than one occasion." He led her now, moving down the wide, shallow steps of the verandah and into the garden.

"I love the night sky in the country. It's so wide and I can see the stars. In London, I can't see anything at night. The sky is blocked out with all the pollution and chimney smoke." Alasdair positioned himself behind Marianne and pointed to a cluster of stars. "That's Cassiopeia. Once you find that constellation, you can use it as a reference point to find the other constellations. Look, there's Ursa Major and the North Star." He raised his arm and gestured with his hand as if drawing an invisible line that connected the stars.

"I had no idea you were such a scientist, Alasdair. First the gaslights and now the constellations."

He laughed. "You seem unduly surprised."

"You didn't mention any of this in London." Marianne turned to face him, her hand playfully resting on the lapels of his evening coat. The gesture bespoke a warming familiarity and was, of course, not the type of gesture an English girl would use at all, for it was far too intimate for English tastes. But not for his. "There's apparently a lot I don't know about you, Alasdair, so many layers. I'm intrigued about what else I might learn."

The comment itself was far too flirtatious by English standards with its veiled invitation to seduction.

Marianne clearly had not meant to imply that she was open to any untoward overtures. Nonetheless, Alasdair was overwhelmed. He could not recall if there'd ever been anyone, let alone a woman, who'd been interested enough to get to know him and his many "layers" as Marianne had put it.

The light atmosphere which had surrounded their earlier conversation changed into something serious, something tender. "No one has ever wanted to look that deeply at me before, Marianne." The world had slowed for him, each minute detail becoming brilliantly apparent to his senses. He could smell the lemon-lavender scent of her soap at this close distance, see the small race of her pulse at the base of her neck.

Marianne's brow furrowed slightly as if she could not quite grasp the concept that someone *wouldn't* want to look deeper.

"The truth is, Marianne, almost everyone who knows me sees only Viscount Pennington. My only worth is in being the flesh-and-blood incarnation of the family title. I'm nothing but a rich, well-educated, perhaps-pampered male whose only duty is to stand to stud and continue the incarnation for future generations." He hadn't meant to sound so utterly cynical, but once he'd started, the words had poured out unedited and harsh. Marianne blushed at the last but stood her ground, unabashed by his candor. He feared for a moment that he might have earned her scorn, or even her pity. But Marianne bit her lower lip thoughtfully, considering her words before replying. It was a great consolation that he knew without equivocation her words would be sincere and not a knee-jerk reaction of platitudes.

She shook her head in the moonlight, making her hair appear like an ethereal halo. "It's ironic, then, that I've never seen you that way. You've never been 'the viscount' to me up until today when we arrived. It wasn't until I saw you standing on the front steps, surrounded by the trappings of this house, that I realized it."

"You have no idea how potent that concept is, the notion of being looked upon as a man and nothing more," Alasdair whispered, his voice hoarse with barely contained desire.

"It is all anyone wants," Marianne replied softly, her eyes never leaving his. "You no more want to be cherished for your title than I want to be cherished for my fortune."

Was that a warning or a wish? Alasdair heard both in her soft tones. She smiled fondly at him to indicate she meant no malice with her words, and then she stepped away from him, letting go of his lapels, moving out of reach. "Good night, Alasdair. Don't stay out too long." The ivory silk of her gown had a luminosity of its own as she moved over the yard and back to the terrace like a floating angel, leaving Alasdair to ponder the thoughts she had shared with him.

The intuition that had drawn him to Marianne from the first had proven to be right. He knew with the most primal of instincts that Marianne was meant for him.

His need for her had been revealed tonight with shocking clarity. It was quite simple and straightforward. He cared for her and she was not indifferent to him in a romantic sense. Beyond that, she'd displayed a level of understanding that overwhelmed him. And yet, the simple path that should be taken at this juncture was full of twists and turns.

He had to ensure that Marianne knew that the depth of his affection ran much deeper than her father's fortune, that he cared for her precisely because of who she was inside.

If it was up to him, he'd propose outright and marry her as fast as he could. But that was far too precipitous, especially when she might decide that the burden of his mother's dislike was too much to bear in exchange for what he offered her. That was a question worth pondering. What did he have to offer Marianne Addison, a girl who had everything?

He had an expensive estate that could no longer support itself with its tenant rents. He had an overbearing mother who would not relinquish the household reins without a struggle. He had a high-priced friendship with the Prince of Wales, a friendship that sucked his coffers as dry as his estate did. Marianne would see all that; she was too smart not to. And she would wonder how much of his courtship was, indeed, predicated on the worth of her dowry and how much was based on genuine affection. Would he ever be able to convince her that his heart was enough?

Alasdair raised his head to the night sky and drew a deep breath. No one had ever mentioned how difficult it was to court an heiress. The money seemed to get in the way.

Chapter Twelve

The days before the prince's arrival were a frenzy of activity. Tradesmen and workmen from the village swarmed the length and breadth of Highborough from the gardens to the garrets where trunks of carefully packed linens and expensive bed curtains were being unearthed and placed in chambers that had, until recently, housed bare bed frames.

"It's almost as if the house is putting on a ball gown or a grand costume," Marianne remarked to Alasdair while they wrestled a trunk into large bedchamber.

"It's the aristocratic version of economizing," Alasdair said wryly, tugging loose the wide leather straps that had been holding the trunk shut. "It's an expensive honor to entertain the prince. Some people spend a year getting ready for his visit. One lady I know even

155

built a special conservatory just for the royal visit." Alasdair threw back the heavy lid. A strong scent of lavender and rue filled the air almost immediately.

Marianne reached through layers of tissue paper and pulled out the sheets on top. She shook out the exquisitely hemmed Irish linen. "No stains. The trunk has preserved them beautifully but they'll have to be pressed."

"I haven't found a way to prevent wrinkles yet." Alasdair took the linen from her and studied it.

Marianne stared into the trunk so reminiscent of the trunks that had contained her dresses from Worth. An idea came to her. "When everything is packed up next time, we should try to emulate Worth's packing methods. They ship dresses across the Atlantic and the gowns arrive without being crushed. I think it's due to the layers of bedding he uses to cushion the gowns and keep them from wrinkling," Marianne suggested.

Alasdair gave her a queer look. For a moment she wondered if she'd said something wrong. Then his face split into a wide smile and an intangible spark connected them in that moment. "I do believe you've got something there. We'll try it. If it works, you will have won the housekeeper's admiration forever. She's got three girls from the village down there right now doing nothing but pressing linens. Goodness knows we could put those girls to better use if we could spare them."

Marianne smiled back, a butterfly of excitement

making a small flutter in her stomach. She enjoyed working with Alasdair. Doing a project with him was quite different than strolling through London or perusing the bookshelves of Hatchards or dancing with him at a ball. This was real work; they were creating something from their efforts. When they finished with a trunk, a room was transformed into a lovely vision.

A maid popped into the room, loaded down with a basket of freshly pressed linens. Marianne traded her the clean linen for the wrinkled. She snapped open a sheet, laughing as Alasdair struggled to catch the fluttering ends that came his way.

"Surely you don't expect me to make this bed up?" Alasdair asked, laughter in his tone at being overcome by quantities of flowing white linen.

"Surely I do, sirrah," Marianne scolded playfully, dragging her edge of the sheet to the far side of the massive bed. She smoothed the sheet onto the mattress and began to tuck it neatly under the mattress edge. However, she noted that Alasdair had stopped, his side of the linen hanging down to the floor. "You have to tuck it under," Marianne explained.

"Ah, of course." Alasdair set about tucking, but she saw immediately that his tucking more closely resembled stuffing.

"Stop." Marianne put her hands on her hips and faced him squarely. "Have you ever actually made up a bed?"

"Not that I can recall, frankly." Alasdair's voice carried a tone of humility to it but his eyes were full of mocking mischief. He was trying not to laugh.

Marianne gave in to mirth at the sight of his boyish penitence. "Alasdair Braden, I declare, you are hopeless." She shook her head.

"Well, there is one thing I am good at in the bedroom," he said with a seriousness that took Marianne entirely off guard. She wasn't sure how to reply to that. Surely he didn't mean to imply what she was thinking.

She decided to play it cool. "And what, precisely, is that?"

"Why, it's pillow fights, of course. What did you think I meant?" His eyes widened in deliberate innocence. "Why, Marianne Addison, were you having impure thoughts? I have just the cure. We'll beat them out of you." In one lightning movement Alasdair swooped up a pillow from the pile on the floor and fired it across the wide bed.

Marianne gave a little scream and nimbly dodged the feather bullet. She grabbed up her skirts and jumped onto the bed, making straight for the pile of pillows.

War ensued.

She grabbed a pillow and pummeled Alasdair with it while he tried, only somewhat successfully, to use his pillow as a shield.

"Dear Lord, you're a virago!" Alasdair exclaimed as feathers flew in the chamber above his head.

Marianne was laughing too hard to see his next

move until it was too late. Alasdair gave up his pillow shield and charged her like a bull, catching her about the waist and bearing her down on the mattress, thereby forcing her pillow to fly out of her grasp. Alasdair pinned her to the bed, both of them gasping for breath after their laughter and exertions.

"Cry mercy, minx." Alasdair laid down his terms of surrender.

Marianne drew a deep breath, her lack of air having nothing to do any longer with the exertions of their pillow fight and everything to do with the proximity of Alasdair's body to hers. She could see the amusement in his dark eyes and something else too—perhaps desire looked like that, like he would devour her if he could. There was something dangerous and tempting in that notion. For a second, she thought he would kiss her, and maybe he would have if Audrey hadn't intervened in such a timely fashion.

"What is going on in here? I heard all the commotion downstairs . . ." Audrey's teasing tone faded at the sight of them. "Oh, excuse me," she faltered uncharacteristically. She recovered the next moment, all efficient action.

"Alasdair, get up. Do you want your mother to catch you like that? She's on her way up. You're lucky I'm faster on the stairs than she is."

"We were having a pillow fight," Alasdair explained defensively. He released Marianne and climbed off the bed. "We were doing nothing wrong—just having a little fun, Aud. Being caught having a pillow fight is hardly the same as being caught in flagrante delicto." Alasdair gave an awkward cough. "Ah, hello Sarah, I suppose you heard the noise too." Sarah Stewart's dark head appeared in the door frame behind Audrey's auburn curls.

Marianne sat up. She could see Sarah's eyes darting from her to Alasdair, her mind clearly working to piece together the episode. Marianne winced as Sarah came to the most obvious and correct conclusion: a pillow fight, certainly—the feathers were evidence of that— but a pillow fight that had gone a bit too far and that might have gone even farther if they'd been allowed to follow the course of things.

Marianne was swamped with guilt. Perhaps she imagined a look of hurt sweep Sarah's features briefly, or perhaps it really had. While she knew Alasdair's feelings in regard to Sarah, she had not ascertained the true depth of Sarah's feelings toward Alasdair. She'd thought Sarah looked upon Alasdair with the affection of a friend last night, but it was entirely possible she'd seen what she wanted to see, what she wanted to believe. Sarah had stood as her friend, welcoming her openly last night. Marianne owed her better than this.

Marianne slid off the bed and began repairing the damage to the rumpled sheet. Alasdair's mother could be heard coming down the hall.

"What has happened here? We're supposed to be getting the rooms ready, not destroying them," she huffed. "It's bad enough we have to do anything at all." She'd been sorely put out by Audrey's suggestion, that morning, that every hand available should pitch in to help ready Highborough for the impending royal visit.

She threw up her hands in disgust. "This is what happens when one asks a viscount to make a bed."

"It won't take long to clean this up," Marianne said, already pushing the loose feathers into a pile with her hands.

"We'll leave you to it," Audrey replied, shooting her a sharp look that Marianne could not dismiss. "All right, everyone back to your projects." She made a shooing motion with her hands and dispersed the little group, leaving Marianne and Alasdair alone.

"I'm sorry," Alasdair began, once more the reserved Englishman who'd met her on the steps.

"Don't be." Marianne smiled. "That is, unless you didn't think it was fun?"

His reserve melted. "Well played, Marianne. It was great fun. It's not every day a viscount gets to engage in all-out pillow warfare."

"Nor is it every day a viscount learns to make a bed." Marianne eyed the half-made bed with serious intent. "Back to work. I believe we left off with tucking. Not stuffing, mind you, tucking."

They worked companionably after that, finishing

the bed and laying linen towels out for the guest who would occupy that room during the house party.

Marianne fluffed the last pillow and stepped back to survey their handiwork.

"Does it pass inspection?" Alasdair asked, coming to her side.

"Yes, it does. You've done well for a beginner."

"We make a good team, Marianne," he said quietly, all teasing gone from his tone and his eyes.

"Thank you," Marianne responded in kind.

"Marianne, may I kiss you? I find myself quite suddenly overwhelmed by your domestic talents."

Marianne shook her head, and her hand pressed his. "No, it wouldn't be right. There are things to be sorted out with Sarah first. I couldn't kiss you knowing that our being together has caused her pain," Marianne said softly, hoping Alasdair understood.

"Sarah and I talked before your arrival. She has no expectations of me. I've told her I will not be pursuing her hand. She assured me she was relieved to hear it."

"What else was she to say? Was she to throw a tantrum? She knew there was nothing she could do to dissuade you from your decision. A lady could do nothing more than prove appreciative of your plans." Marianne touched his arm lightly. "I'll speak with her after lunch. It will make me feel better."

In the drowsy hours of the afternoon, Sarah and Marianne strolled the parkland that led out to the

Highborough summerhouse. The others had succumbed to the warm afternoon and were resting, except for Alasdair whom they'd left on the back terrace with a book.

"I am sorry about this morning," Marianne began, idly picking a meadow wildflower that grew along the path.

Sarah pretended ignorance. "Sorry for what?"

"For the pillow fight," Marianne said bluntly.

Sarah tried to dismiss her efforts. "No one should have to apologize for having a little fun."

"Don't do that, Sarah." Marianne came to a stop in the path and faced her new friend. "Don't pretend that you didn't understand the scene fully. The pillow fight became something substantially more than its original intent."

Sarah said nothing and they walked a ways in silence. When it became apparent that Sarah would not venture anything further in the conversation, Marianne said, "I know there was talk of you and Alasdair marrying."

"There was only ever talk, nothing more." Sarah's face sported a wistful smile. "He has informed me most politely that his intentions do not lie in that direction."

"I am sorry. I feel as if it's my fault." Marianne felt wretched. She and Alasdair had fallen in love. They could not help it, and in truth, she hadn't known of the situation with Sarah until it had become too late to withdraw her affections.

Sarah put a gentle hand on Marianne's arm. "My dear, it's not your fault. You didn't cause him not to want to marry me. He's never wanted to marry me. You haven't changed that. I've always known he's been a rather reluctant but polite suitor."

But Marianne sensed he was the only reluctant party. Sarah had not once mentioned her relief. "But you care for him," Marianne boldly ventured.

Sarah gave a wide smile that took Marianne by surprise. "How could I not love Alasdair? Who doesn't love him? He's handsome and kind and full of life. He's gallant and fun loving when he has the chance. He's the sun around which we all revolve. The truth is, I've been worried for him the past few years. There's a darker edge to him than there used to be, and I can't make him happy. I can't take that dark edge away. But you can. I can see it when he's with you, and you're all he talked about this past week." Sarah gave her a beseeching look. "I think, for the first time in his life, Alasdair is discovering that he needs someone."

Marianne knew what Sarah meant about that darker edge. She'd seen it too, that day at the Tower and here at Highborough, for brief moments. "I've come to care for Alasdair during our short association in London but I can't countenance the idea of my happiness being made by stealing another's," Marianne confessed.

Sarah squeezed Marianne's hand affectionately. "Then you are as thoughtful as Alasdair told me." She leaned toward Marianne as they walked, as if they were conspirators. "He told me that you went into a duck pond in Hyde Park to retrieve a little boy's boat because you couldn't stand his tears. I thought someone who did that must be quite kindhearted."

Marianne blushed. "I ruined my stockings but it was a small price to pay to see the little boy grin."

"I'm glad Alasdair has found you, Marianne. Perhaps I am even a bit relieved. I've spent my whole adult life living under the onus of knowing that I was expected to marry him. It was not an unpleasant burden. He would never have been unkind to me and we would have made a companionable go of things. But the burden was in knowing that Alasdair was merely settling for me and that I could not truly make him happy, although he'd never admit it. We would have spent our lives trying to do the impossible for each other and never succeeding." Sarah looked down at her hands. "May I tell you something? Many might consider it highly controversial. Perhaps you won't."

Marianne nodded, hardly able to imagine what Sarah Stewart would have to say that would qualify as scandalous.

Sarah's voice dropped to a near whisper even though they were entirely alone out-of-doors. "I think the day of the aristocrat is fading. Alasdair thinks so too. I help my father with the ledgers and I see physical proof in those columns that estates can no longer maintain themselves living off the rents of their tenants. It's not a passing consideration that will be outgrown. It's the way of things now. What defines a gentleman's lifestyle is changing. I think you're someone who can help Alasdair find a way to bridge that gap. In fact, I think you're exactly the person to do it."

A thought crossed Marianne's mind at Sarah's resounding endorsement. Sarah had spent years thinking her adult life would come to a particular end and now, relieved or not, that expected outcome had been removed. "What about you? Have you given a thought to your future?"

A slow, coy smile spread across Sarah's face, making her look more lively, quite pretty in fact, in marked contrast to the girl who had blended in with the draperies earlier that week. "Perhaps I might travel after all. I should love to see your San Francisco. Then again, I might find someone of my own to care for without worrying if it's good for the estate." The way she said it, Marianne thought she might already have someone in mind. It occurred to Marianne that Sarah might have had someone in mind for quite some time but could not act on it out of loyalty to Alasdair and her father's expectations.

"How will your father take the news?" Marianne ventured to ask. She already knew how Alasdair's mother would react, how Alasdair's mother was already reacting to her mere presence in the house.

"He'll manage. It will be a harder adjustment for him. He and Alasdair's mother have had their plans for quite some time. They've been quite keen to join the estates and the families." Sarah shrugged. "They've both been alone for years and I understand how appealing it would be to create a whole family of sorts again, to feel part of something. I think they thought they'd have that if Alasdair and I married—their very own country dynasty."

"If that's so, maybe they should marry each other," Marianne said.

Sarah giggled. "Now, there's an idea."

The mood at the table that evening was boisterous, the good cheer nearly palpable as they all sat down at the table. Everyone had worked hard the past few days, and the prince would arrive tomorrow along with the other guests. The good cheer had a punchy quality to it, no doubt from everyone's weariness, but Highborough was ready.

Linens were pressed; beds with their luxury sheeting were made up; rooms smelled fresh and clean. Carpets had been rolled out in public rooms and draperies beaten dust free. For Marianne's part, her good humor stemmed from the walk with Sarah. She had not realized how heavily her concern over Sarah's reaction had weighed on her. It had been cathartic to hear Sarah's reassurances and to know that she was not merely stepping aside, but that she was relieved to get on with her life in a happier venue.

After dinner, the men did not sit at the table for port and the group did not seem inclined to linger over the tea trolley, their efforts over the past several days catching up to them. Marianne noticed that all Audrey had to do was stifle a small yawn behind her hand and everyone quickly rose and said their good nights before eagerly seeking their chambers.

"Might I have a word with you before you go up?" Alasdair asked quietly at her side as the others filed past them.

The soft, private quality of his voice sent a delicious thrill down her spine. "Of course."

Marianne's mother kissed her cheek on her way up. "Don't be long, darling. It will be an early day tomorrow."

When the last of the group had gone upstairs, Alasdair drew her outside to the terrace where they'd walked the first night. He stood next to her, his elbows resting on the carved-stone balustrade, looking out over the gardens with their gaslights. "Do you like it here, Marianne?"

"Your home is astonishing. It's like a palace," Marianne said truthfully. "But, like a palace, it's not really a place for living. It's a place for showing."

Alasdair made a good-humored grimace. "Ouch, that's quite a comment. I don't think Highborough has ever endured such a blistering set down. But I won't say you're wrong." He reached for her hand, a gesture he'd done so often since they'd met that Marianne marveled it hadn't become commonplace in its effect on her. But, each time, she still thrilled to it, gloves and all.

Alasdair looked down at her gloved hand in his. "Highborough is like your hand, gloved and displayed for all to see but not to touch, not really. For once, I'd like to hold your hand, your real hand, and all these conventions be hanged."

"I think that can be arranged." Marianne slipped her hand from his and began to peel off her long gloves. "What about Highborough, Alasdair? Can it take off its gloves? Metaphorically speaking of course."

A wistful look crossed his features. "I think that's up to you. If anyone can make Highborough less of a mausoleum it would be you," he said, reaching for her bared hand and tracing a delicate circle in the center of her palm. Marianne felt herself give a silly tremble. It seemed ridiculous to react so thoroughly to a simple touch of a finger. But it wasn't just any finger—it was Alasdair's—and his touch alone had affected her this way since the beginning of their time together.

"I'm not certain I understand," Marianne replied honestly. It was hard to understand anything when the whole of her body and mind were intent on what Alasdair was doing to her hand.

Alasdair flashed her a boyish grin. "Marianne, there's something I want to ask you."

What an ominous phrase. Marianne's stomach flipped and she fought the urge to sit down. *Oh Lord,* she thought. *This is it.*

Chapter Thirteen

"Do you know why a gentleman invites a lady to his country home? To see the 'old pile,' as it were?"

The question caught her entirely off guard. "No, I am afraid not, unless it's to help him clean house or for pillow fights."

Alasdair gave a small shake of his head, and Marianne immediately regretted her attempt at levity. With a serious gesture, he drew a small, square box out of his inner coat pocket. "A gentleman invites a lady to his family seat to meet the family, the neighbors, to see the house, to see if she could imagine being mistress of such a place. In short, Marianne, the invitation is a prelude to a marriage proposal." His fingers flicked open the lid of the small velvet box. "I am asking you to marry me, Marianne, to be my countess."

Marianne stared at the ring, utterly speechless.

"I am honored, truly I am," Marianne managed once she'd found her voice. She should have been better prepared than this. Since the day in the boat at Regent's Park she'd known there was a strong likelihood of facing his proposal. She should have been practicing what she'd say, what she'd do.

Alasdair tried for levity, his tone lighthearted. "I have to tell you that the English consider it bad form to reject a proposal at this point in the game. Once we get to the 'old pile' part of the courting process, acceptance is considered a fait accompli."

Marianne laughed. "Oh Alasdair, no girl in her right mind would consider refusing you. Are you sure you want to do this, that I'm the one for all the right reasons?"

Alasdair was all seriousness again. "This is not about money, Marianne. I didn't come here and see the estate last week and think, 'Marianne's money would save me. I'll propose and all will be well.' I came here and I saw a cold, aging house with no life in it. I thought, 'What a waste this pile of brick and pillars is. This is supposed to be a family seat. To me, that means the place should be alive, stuffed to the ceilings with the rowdiness of a family that likes to be together. It's never felt that way to me, not even when my father was alive. But I've craved that in my bones for what seems forever. I can't remember a time when I didn't dream about the kind of family I wanted at Highborough."

Alasdair shook his head. "But when I started looking for a wife, and I was a man who looked in earnest, I couldn't find a woman who could or would share those dreams with me. All they saw was my coronet and my title. So I stopped looking until the night I saw you at the ball. I knew immediately that you were the one." Alasdair drew a deep breath. "I'm rambling. I suppose it's a sign of how desperate I am to have you say yes."

He was teasing her again in his delightful way, in a way that she understood better now. It was something of a shock to realize that she had the ability to unnerve this most-confident of men. Sarah was right: Alasdair had a personality, an easy air, about him that drew others naturally. But Marianne recognized tonight that he was using that easy air to cover his nervousness. She felt it was quite a testament to the truth of his statement that this proposal wasn't motivated by his need for a fortune, but by his sincere regard for her, a regard that she shared.

"I must confess I've not proposed to anyone until tonight, as you may have inferred. Tell me, Marianne, have I made a muddle of my proposal?"

"Not at all. I think it's quite the finest proposal a girl could ever receive." She was still trying to wrap her mind around the lovely image of transforming the cold house into a place of warmth and laughter. "I was just thinking that, with a little more beeswax, the banister would make a great slide."

Alasdair threw back his dark head and laughed wholeheartedly. "Redecorating already. Does this mean you'll say yes?"

Marianne pushed aside any remaining doubts and arguments she could conjure up that would demand she refuse. Those arguments and reasons had nothing to do with the two of them. She recognized now, in a flash of insight, that any of her objections and worries had stemmed from concern over what others thought. There would be people who would never admit that she could live up to a certain standard simply because they didn't want her to. In many ways, she'd always be the outsider. But that was their problem. Alasdair loved her and she loved him—adored him, in fact. The two of them would build a good life together and that was what mattered most. Alasdair loved her for herself and she loved him for something more than his title. In this moment, it was all so simple, so straightforward, so obvious that it seemed silly to have worried about it at all.

With the stars as her witnesses, on the terrace of Highborough, Marianne Addison said yes on the condition that Alasdair promised not tell anyone until the royal visit was over, so as not to take attention away from the prince.

Alasdair agreed and sealed his promise with a kiss.

As with many promises, there were some small infractions. News this exciting could not be kept entirely secret no matter how hard one tried. Marianne quietly confided the next morning to her mother in the morning room, and Alasdair asked for permission to send news of the announcement to the *Times* since the announcement wouldn't reach London and the papers until later in the week.

The prince's arrival defused some of the excitement that burned between Marianne and Alasdair. Prince Albert was a gregarious, social creature, surprisingly affable in conversation. But he had monumental needs, as evidenced by the enormous entourage that traveled with him, and by his extensive wardrobe. "He has more clothes than you have Worth dresses," Alasdair joked with Marianne privately as they watched the royal baggage parade in an unending stream up the staircase.

Joking aside, Marianne could tell that the monarch had a genuine affection for Alasdair and Alasdair for him. Although there was plenty of catering to the man's needs, the relationship between Alasdair and the prince was not based solely on sycophantic kowtowing and the currying of favor. Audrey had kept the guest list small, inviting only the closest of friends. Marianne saw the reason for that now. The prince was polite to all those around him but he enjoyed time alone with Alasdair, walking the grounds or riding out with him.

For Alasdair's part, Marianne noted that he played the host to perfection. With affable ease, he dismissed his efforts behind the scenes in the month prior to the visit. He had all of the prince's favorite delicacies on hand for tea. If Marianne hadn't known better she would not have guessed what an effort it had been to arrange for the cases of Heidsieck champagne and crates of lobster for patties and salads. The amount of food the house party went through astonished Marianne. She couldn't help but wonder if Alasdair kept a mental tally in his head of what his largesse was costing. Not that it mattered. When she married him, she would see that he wanted for nothing, that he never had to think twice about certain economies. He'd said he didn't want her money, but that made her all the more determined to see that he had it. For the first time in a long while, Marianne was glad to be an heiress. Once the announcement was formalized, her father would settle a respectable sum on them and one of Alasdair's worries would be eased.

Although Marianne was eager to announce the engagement, the week of the house party flew by. A wealth of activities had been planned to keep the guests entertained, and the weather cooperated beautifully, allowing all types of outdoor excursions to follies, to the village and to other scenic points of interest. Alasdair had even planned a few "American" activities in honor of the Americans present as well as Bertie's penchant for American pastimes.

At Alasdair's encouragement, Marianne paired up with her father in a team rifle-shooting competition. The prince exclaimed over her prowess with the American guns with which her father traveled. She partnered with Alasdair in the archery tournament and acquitted herself well in the riding demonstration, using a western-style saddle.

"It's so unwieldy," the prince remarked, running his hands over the wide leather expanse of the western saddle. "This saddle horn is enormous."

"It allows a cowboy to carry rope over it for easy access," Marianne explained. Indeed, the saddle did look gigantic compared to the smaller, sculpted English variation.

"The style is more comfortable too," her father put in, joining the group that surrounded Marianne's horse. "Cattlemen spend hours a day in the saddle."

In the evenings, Marianne and the other ladies took turns at the piano. At the prince's insistence, Marianne played band music from America. On some nights, there was dancing. Marianne loved these nights the best since they provided her with a few moments in Alasdair's arms.

At the end of the week, Prince Albert invited the Addison family to join him on his yacht at Cowes. He'd expressed interest in seeing her father's yacht, which was awaiting their arrival for a week of racing there. In short, Marianne thought the house party represented one of the best weeks she'd ever experienced. Alasdair's mother had been too busy fussing over the prince to pay any attention to her. Even if she had turned her attentions toward Marianne, Marianne doubted that Lady

Pennington would have dared to voice any level of disapproval when the prince had so clearly given the young woman his favor.

On the last day of the party, Marianne stood with Audrey and Alasdair and the others on the wide front steps of Highborough, waving off the royal carriages with promises to see the prince the following week in Cowes. Beside her, Alasdair managed a secret squeeze of her hand. She didn't dare risk looking at him, but she smiled, not caring who saw the smile or to what they attributed it. The week had been a triumph, and she'd triumphed along with it.

Lord Brantley threw down his copy of the *Times* with thorough disgust. Pennington had proposed and been accepted. Pennington had been in the countryside entertaining an elite few and the prince while he, Brantley, slaved away in London amid the infinite maze of social events and restrictions, hoping to find enough funds to keep going.

The tables at the gaming hells and card parties had only been marginally lucrative these past weeks and his pockets were feeling the pinch. Pennington's pockets were definitely not feeling the pinch these days. With the assurance of the heiress' fortune behind him, Pennington could entertain the prince without worry.

The American chit had even garnered the prince's affections. That was no surprise—the girl was lovely and the prince was enchanted with American girls. Logically, it all added up. But that didn't stop Brantley from feeling a stab of jealousy. The American would be joining His Royal Highness on his yacht at Cowes, one of the most coveted social invitations one could receive. Of course her father had a yacht. Brantley recalled hearing that he was having one commissioned in Cherbourg especially for the racing.

Brantley snorted and reached for his coffee. The American girl had been plenty smart. She'd planned her campaign. He could see that now. The large town house in a prestigious neighborhood, the endless train of impeccable, formfitting Worth gowns, the sponsorship from the American Countess of Camberly. With her natural beauty and liveliness, it had been too easy to assume the girl had simply fallen into all her good luck and social acceptance by accident. But Brantley thought otherwise. The yacht was the clincher. She or her family had known ahead of time how partial the prince would be to another sporting man if they could just get a chance to meet him.

Paired with the purchase of a yacht ready just in time for the regatta at Cowes, the reasons Marianne Addison had come to London in the first place seemed blatantly obvious. She had been title-hunting in an attempt to get back at, or to escape, the stigma with which she'd been branded in New York for her escapades there.

Brantley had yet to let that bit of information come

to light. The time to do so was upon him, he thought. Pennington's mother couldn't be pleased about the announcement of the engagement between her son and the nouveau riche American chit, since she'd been an overt champion of Sarah Stewart for years. She'd be eager to thwart her son's alliance with Marianne Addison, especially if it meant avoiding a scandal.

Cowes seemed the perfect place to do it. There would be several Americans there, eager to show off their yachts. They would not be warm to the idea that a country woman of theirs who had been snubbed by Mrs. Astor and hadn't managed to gain admittance to the revered Four Hundred Club was now finding success at the highest levels of British society. That alone would start the tongues wagging and Pennington's mother thundering.

But that was all a contingency plan. Brantley didn't truly expect the scandal to break, although he was prepared to go that far. He'd try blackmail first. Pennington was not a stupid man. The viscount would understand the ramifications of this scandal breaking. Pennington would want to take all measures necessary to prevent word from getting out. He wouldn't want to risk the prince's displeasure at having been associated with the Addisons through him, and heaven help him, if Pennington had actually fallen in love with his intended bride, he'd want to protect her too.

Brantley pushed back from the table and headed for his writing desk. He had a letter to write and a trip to plan. He was going to win the wager. Marianne would not last the regatta.

Cowes, the Isle of Wight

In the privacy of the room serving as an office at the rented house in Cowes, Alasdair's hand made a fist and crushed the plain white stationery that contained the hateful letter.

He'd been foolish to think that they would remain unscathed. There were only two weeks of the Season left, counting the regatta week, and he'd been too optimistic. He'd also misjudged Brantley. He'd hoped his engagement to Marianne would have signaled to Brantley, as it would have to any other gentleman, that the chase was off. Marianne was officially committed to another. A gentleman knew the rules. It was not acceptable to poach on another's territory. Of course, he couldn't explain it to Marianne in those terms. She would cringe at such a barbaric idea as women being property. But the idea was solid.

Apparently, Brantley wasn't playing by those rules. The man must be more desperate for funds than he'd imagined if Brantley was willing to play such a deep and vile game. This was blatant extortion: three thousand pounds in order to keep Marianne's scandalous escapade from becoming public, whatever that escapade was.

Alasdair didn't know what to think. Audrey had only alluded to it once. He'd never brought it up with

Marianne and she had never brought it into the realm of their conversations. Not knowing made it difficult to ascertain the reasonability of Brantley's price. Had she done something minor that had been blown out of proportion, or had she done something truly upsetting? Knowing Marianne as he did, he rather believed the former.

There was no question of whether or not he should pay the fee. Blackmail had no end once someone gave in, and Brantley would not let it go. If he dared to importune them once, he'd dare it again. Alasdair would not have his marriage plagued by such a shadow, unless the scandal was so horrific that it bore considering such a sacrifice.

Alasdair unfolded the crumpled paper and smoothed it on the surface of his desk. He couldn't go to the authorities. Brantley had been too careful in his choice of words. The threat was veiled, and one would only understand the implication of the words if one knew all the private history and angles between the two of them. Alasdair could sense the dark humor with which Brantley had penned the letter, knowing very well he couldn't go to the authorities and say, "This man is mad at me for spilling champagne on his shirt and stealing a dance."

No, he couldn't go to the authorities. But he could go to Marianne. Before he took any action, he had to know what had happened in New York. He didn't relish the thought of asking her about it any more than he relished the thought of knowing what it was. He couldn't imagine it would be significant enough to alter the way he felt about her. But the whole situation would inherently bring tension into an already fragile relationship where they were still getting to know one another. Perhaps Brantley had known that would be the outcome and this was just one more tactic to drive a wedge between Marianne and Alasdair.

Well, bad news didn't get better by being put off. Alasdair left the office, the note tucked in his pocket, to search out Marianne. The house he'd rented along with Camberly and Lionel and the Addisons was large, large enough to accommodate the three groups without their stepping all over each other. Right now, though, he was cursing the enormous spaces. Marianne wasn't in the conservatory with Audrey. She wasn't in the garden with her mother. She wasn't shooting billiards with Lionel and Camberly, although he hadn't really thought she would be.

The last place he checked was the library, where he found Stella penning letters. "She's not here, Dair." Stella looked up from her stationery. "She was, though. We were going through the correspondence together. She got up suddenly and said something about going to the kitchen." Stella paused. "I hope that makes sense? I don't know what she's up to, but I rather thought a letter upset her, although she didn't say anything specific."

Alasdair's heart pounded. Had the bastard Brantley threatened her too? The blackguard couldn't leave well enough alone and simply blackmail him, one man to another? To threaten Marianne was reprehensible, entirely beyond any gentleman's code of conduct no matter how loosely written.

Alasdair flew down the stairs to the kitchen, worry and anger in every stride. If Brantley had threatened Marianne directly, the man would live to sorely regret it. When he got done with Brantley, the bloody nose he'd given the journalist would look like a minor infraction.

Chapter Fourteen

The sight that greeted Alasdair in the kitchen caused him to pause in the doorway and stare in amazement. Marianne stood at the long worktable, hands immersed in a deep pile of dough, flour dusting her hair and streaking her face. If it had been anyone else, Alasdair would have thought the scene ridiculous in the extreme. But it was Marianne, and the sight of her baking bread when there were countless other servants who could do the task seemed perfectly natural. He would expect nothing less from his future countess.

In spite of his worry over the current situation, a smile spread across his face at the unorthodox idea of finding Marianne in his kitchens, baking bread, surrounded at some point by their children perched on high stools learning to do the same. Reluctantly, he

185

pushed aside the coveted image of that family. That would be in the future. Right now he had to take care of the present.

Marianne pummeled the round of dough in front of her. The stern concentration etched on her face suggested he'd been right in his initial assumption. Brantley had sent her a letter as well.

Alasdair pushed off the door frame and made his presence known with a little cough. "What are you doing, Marianne?" he asked in friendly tones although he knew perfectly well what she was doing.

Marianne looked up, startled at the intrusion. "I'm making bread." Alasdair heard the wariness in her tone. "It's what I do when I have a problem to solve or something that bothers me."

Alasdair pulled up a tall wooden stool and sat at the counter. "Lord Brantley has sent me a note and I am guessing that he sent one to you too."

Marianne bit her bottom lip. "Yes. Mine came in the post this morning." She shook her head. "I shouldn't have let myself be so happy last week. Everything was wonderful and now this will ruin it all."

"How could it possibly ruin everything?"

She paused from her bread punching and fixed him with a strong gaze. "I won't let you pay him, Alasdair. Paying his fee only validates for him that he possesses information that has value."

Alasdair nodded. "I had no intentions, nor I hope do you, of paying for his silence."

"He will tell everyone what happened in New York," Marianne said quietly, absently massaging a bit of dough that had become separated from the pile.

"Probably," Alasdair agreed. "Is it all that bad if he does? We'll still be married as we planned. We'll still turn Highborough into the home I want it to be. There is very little he could say that would alter our plans, Marianne. I am not sure he understands that or he would know what an outlandish gamble he's taking. He would know the odds are against him in terms of succeeding with his course of action."

Marianne smiled at his encouraging words. He, too, felt bolstered by them. It was true, he realized. He had no intention of letting this measly piece of blackmail alter what he'd waited to find his whole life. The world became a simpler place when one could cut out the extraneous concern about what others would think and focus on one's own priorities. The only reason he cared about Brantley's threat was that he didn't want to see Marianne hurt.

Alasdair reached for a clump of dough and took off his coat. He began rolling up the sleeves of his very white shirt. "Does this really work for relieving stress?"

"It works for me." Marianne studied him with acute disbelief. "What are you doing?"

"I'm going to try it. I have to admit I've never kneaded bread before, but until last week, I'd never made a bed either." Alasdair kept his tone purposely light. "While I'm learning, perhaps you can tell me what happened in New York that would have Brantley believing he could blackmail you."

Marianne sobered. "There will be a scandal, Alasdair, if word gets out. Your mother won't like it."

Alasdair gave a harsh laugh. His mother had been poleaxed by the official announcement of his engagement before the party had left Highborough. She'd been so thoroughly upset by the notion that she'd refused to accompany the group to Cowes. "Then the scandal won't change anything," he said nonchalantly. He'd come to terms with his disappointing relationship with his mother years ago, and although he was always optimistic that relationship could be changed if she desired it, he wasn't always hopeful. His choosing Marianne for a wife was only one of many things they had disagreed on over the years.

"Tell me your story, Marianne, and let me be the judge of it." Alasdair gave his dough an experimental punch. "I'm ready for it."

"New York was exciting. There was so much to see, and people were friendly. My mother's family is from New England and they had some connections. I had a sponsor in New York. It helped immensely. I'd been told in advance that New Yorkers looked down their noses at new money, especially at fortunes that came out of the West. San Francisco and Denver are cities that are too raw for their tastes. But since I had a sponsor, no one cared overmuch about my 'questionable' antecedents." Marianne reached across the work-table. "Try it like this," she suggested, guiding Alasdair's hands in a more-regular motion.

"Within a week I had a group of young friends with whom I went everywhere. We attended the same functions. Their families invited my mother and me to sit in their opera boxes, to come to their country houses for a winter weekend on the Hudson . . . One of my new friends was a girl named Rachel. Another young man in our set, Christopher Archer, had also become a close friend of mine. He made certain to dance with me at parties and I thought the three of us formed a very nice trio."

"Let me guess," Alasdair broke in. "Rachel didn't think so."

"Exactly. I didn't know that there was an understanding of sorts between Christopher and Rachel. Apparently, this understanding had been arranged between their families for ages." Marianne huffed. "We don't do things that way in San Francisco. For one thing, the city's not old enough to have families that can trace their roots back for a century."

The parallel to the situation with Sarah could not have been more obvious. Alasdair nodded his head. He saw now why she'd been so concerned, early in their relationship, about the rumor regarding his unofficial status with Sarah Stewart. She'd recently come out of a similar situation. It made her reluctance to pursue a courtship with him perfectly understandable, and admirable even, seeing that she would put the concerns of another ahead of her own happiness.

"Rachel told me about Champagne Sundays and arranged for me to attend one of them."

"Wait, what's a Champagne Sunday?" Alasdair queried.

"Well, Sundays are the most boring days of the week in New York. Proper homes don't receive on Sundays and no events are held. But other ladies, who live on the fringes of social acceptance, discovered this was a vacuum that they could fill with social events of their own. So, on Sundays, these ladies would invite men of their acquaintance to their homes. They would serve champagne. Sometimes there'd be an oyster dinner or a visiting opera singer who performed. There would oftentimes be singing and dancing."

Alasdair nodded. He grasped the concept, something a bit akin to the demimonde of London but on a smaller scale.

"I didn't fully understand the implications of attending a Champagne Sunday. At the time, it seemed like a fun lark, a harmless dare. The activities weren't exactly of a debauched nature—only the company was. I suddenly learned in New York that it didn't matter so much what you did but who you did it with. I could eat oysters at Delmonico's without repercussion, but as soon as I ate oysters in the company of questionable companions on a Sunday, there were consequences."

Alasdair followed the story to its logical conclusion.

"New York ousted you for it, all because you danced too many times with the wrong young man."

"Precisely." Marianne shook her head. "Only it will look so much worse when Lord Brantley tells the story."

Alasdair could see that too. Brantley would emphasize that she'd been in the company of men and their mistresses, while champagne had flowed freely. He would imply that all nature of licentiousness took place.

He pounded at his dough, not so much out of the original frustration he'd felt when he'd first read Brantley's missive, but out of the need to think. After a while, he stopped pounding, pleased to see that a neatly shaped round circle had been formed from his efforts. "I think you're right, Marianne," he said slowly, thinking out loud as an idea took shape. "Brantley feels that he can maximize the story, exaggerate certain parts of it. But if the story can be maximized, perhaps it can also be minimized if we play our cards right."

"How should we go about doing that?" Marianne asked, the wheels of her own mind beginning to spin, the process visible on her face.

Alasdair gave her a wicked grin. "We have to tell the story first. His mistake all along has been assuming we don't want the story to get out. Brantley can't claim blackmail if there is no secret to hide."

Marianne dressed carefully for dinner that night. All of them were joining the Prince of Wales on his yacht for an intimate dinner, a very rare invitation. The setting suited them perfectly. They'd all agreed to "announce" Marianne's New York situation at the supper. After a quick meeting that afternoon, the five friends had convinced Marianne that the prince would be most sympathetic to her plight and eager to champion her side of the story.

Still, she was nervous. Alasdair had reassured her the strategy was perfect and that his feelings for her were not in the least bit altered by this revelation. Marianne took a final look in the long mirror. Tonight she wanted to exude an aura of confidence and she hoped the cream satin gown with its bold rose print would help to accomplish that.

A knock sounded at her door and she gathered up her matching evening wrap and reticule, expecting to find her mother waiting on the other side of the door. But when she opened it, it was to find Alasdair there.

"The others are downstairs and I thought I would fetch you myself. You look stunning." He smiled his appreciation.

"Thank you. I could say the same about you," Marianne replied, taking in the handsome man standing in front of her in evening dress. She never tired of looking at Alasdair. She'd not really paid attention to a man's physique until she'd met him, to the strength inspired by broad shoulders that tapered to a narrow waist, the grace of his long legs. But it was no wonder she'd not noticed the magic of man's body before. So many men were simply not worth the notice that no one had stood out the way he stood out to her.

Alasdair gently took her wrap from her hands and draped it about her shoulders. "What's that in your hair?"

"Do you like it? It's a strand of coral and pearls I had strung to go with this gown in Paris. The coral is supposed to match the roses in the pattern." Marianne raised a hand to touch the jeweled chain woven through her coiffure.

"It's gorgeous. The coral twinkles so subtly in your hair, it makes a man look twice to make sure he's not imagining things." He paused, his eyes starting to spark with the familiar glint of mischief she'd come to associate with him. "I came up here for another reason too, you know."

"What was that?" Marianne played along, tilting her head coquettishly.

"I wanted to steal a kiss."

"I am afraid that will be quite impossible," she said in a tone that caused him a moment's consternation.

"Why is that?"

She tapped him on the nose. "Because you can't steal something that is freely given. You've been doing far too much of the kissing lately. Tonight, it's my turn." With that, Marianne stretched up on her tiptoes and pressed a gentle kiss to his lips.

"What did I do to deserve that most wonderful gift?" Alasdair asked a little later as they descended the stairs.

She shot him a sideways glance. "You believe in me. You love me for what I am and for what I am not."

The night weather at Cowes provided an ideal accompaniment to the dinner cruise. Stars winked overhead and the water was calm beneath them, allowing a table to be set up on the open deck. There had been the requisite tour of the prince's yacht, and dinner conversation had naturally focused on the upcoming regatta. Prince Albert's nephew, Kaiser Wilhelm II, had brought his yacht, *Meteor*, to race for the cup and for the bragging right to be called the King of Cowes.

"He once accused me of sailing with my tailor," the prince said good-naturedly toward the end of the meal. "My boat was out of commission that year, and I was so determined to race that I joined my tailor on his boat. Camberly here has crewed with me before." The prince gestured to the earl who nodded. "I am hoping to persuade you to join me again, Camberly. What do you say?"

"I would be delighted."

"And you, Pennington?" the prince challenged jokingly. "Where will your loyalties lie this year? With your father-in-law-to-be and his new yacht, or with me, your stalwart, longtime friend?"

"That is a difficult decision indeed. I shall have to

ponder it," Alasdair replied easily. Marianne blushed as he caught her eye over the table. Perhaps she'd been too bold with her kiss on the stairs but she'd wanted to kiss him, wanted him to know how she felt, how she understood everything he was endeavoring to do for her.

He should know from the start that she would not be like so many of the wives she'd seen during her time in England, who said nothing, who never spoke of their feelings but merely accepted decisions that were made for them. She would never be that kind of wife.

"Ah, very good." The prince laughed. "It's a smart man who knows how to weigh the influence of his in-laws."

"Speaking of influence," Alasdair began. Marianne was instantly alert to the shift in the conversation. "We have had a slight issue with a dubious character who is seeking to besmirch Miss Addison's reputation by making too much of an unfortunate incident in New York last year."

The prince's eyes narrowed. "Who might this character be?"

"Lord Brantley," Alasdair said unflinchingly.

The prince looked severe. "He's not the best sort, from what I've heard. What has he accused Miss Addison of doing?"

Marianne let Alasdair repeat the tale, knowing that it was better to let him persuade the prince. He made a good telling of it, leaving nothing out. When Alasdair finished his explanation, the prince wiped his mouth with a napkin and leaned back in his chair. "A Champagne Sunday, Miss Addison?" For a moment, Marianne thought she'd be scolded. They'd gambled on the prince's sympathies and lost. Then his face broke into a grin and he gave a hearty chuckle. "It sounds to me like the only scandal there was that they didn't serve Heidsieck's."

The table burst into laughter. Marianne laughed with relief. Brantley would have no hold on them now. Across from her, Alasdair smiled and mouthed the playful words "I told you so." And so he had. He'd told her it would be all right and it was.

Chapter Fifteen

"**D**id you hear what everyone is saying about Miss Addison's escapade in New York?" Brantley groused to Lord Hamsford, his companion at a small tavern in West Cowes.

"You're going to lose the bet." His companion couldn't resist the obvious dig. "The regatta is tomorrow and that's the deadline we set, I believe."

Brantley shook his head in disbelief. Somewhere along the way the bet had become a secondary motivation for him. He was beyond desperate for cash, and his anger at Pennington had grown exponentially with his accumulated debt. By now, he'd thoroughly convinced himself that his circumstances were entirely Pennington's fault. If the Addison chit had danced with him instead, as intended, she would be marrying him now instead of the high-flying viscount.

Pennington had bested him at every turn. Pennington had stolen the heiress out from under him. Pennington had made the little madcap from America respectable even when she waded in duck ponds and made unpopular comments at grand teas. Now, Pennington had even contrived to steal his latest thunder by blowing his blackmail strategy out of the water, and Pennington had done it in great style sitting at the prince's table.

That was another axe he had to grind with Pennington. It galled Brantley to no end that Pennington was about to escape the noose of poverty with his marriage, while he, Brantley, had to continue suffering in curtailed financial straits. It seemed patently unfair.

"You have to admit, the comment was hilarious. 'The only scandal is that they didn't serve Heidsieck's,' " Brantley's companion chortled, mimicking the prince.

Brantley shot him a dark look. "Shut up." If he heard the prince's latest witticism repeated once more he'd punch the next messenger in the nose. Thanks to the prince, no one of account much cared that Marianne Addison had attended a Champagne Sunday in the company of less-reputable members of society. Brantley was astute enough to know that the only ones who did care were the sulky Americans who didn't like the idea of a rejected member of their own society doing so well across the pond in admittedly more-developed social circles than their own. Englishmen would hardly care what their American cousins thought, since they, too, were only outsiders who would eventually go home.

Brantley's last ploy had failed miserably. Instead of ousting the heiress from Society, his actions had only served to entrench her more firmly. Like the Countess of Camberly, she was on her way to becoming accepted.

Sensing his rather-obvious black mood, Brantley's companion left the table so that he could grouse in solitude.

Actually, he wasn't grousing just yet; he was still planning. There had to be a way to spoil Pennington's success and get back a little of his own. Perhaps he'd gone about it the wrong way. He'd been too focused on what supposedly "ruined" American reputations. Brantley slapped his hand on the hard wood planking of the table. He had it!

He would ruin Miss Addison in the most English of ways possible, and he'd do it tomorrow at the regatta. It would be the perfect cover, because when everyone was looking, no one saw a thing.

Blue sky, peppered with the right amount of white clouds to make a decent breeze on The Solent, greeted the sailors and their yachts as they lined up to begin the races. These were no ordinary sailors and deckhands. Boat racing in all its forms, from sailboats to steamer yachts, was the latest rage to sweep Europe. Nobility came from all variety of countries to race in the Cowes regatta, their boats crewed by their noble friends who also shared their passion.

On board the Addison yacht, moored to a spectator pier for the day, Audrey and the Carringtons joined Marianne's family to watch Camberly and Alasdair crew the prince's sailing boat. Marianne and the others held binoculars to their eyes to make out the specific figures on board the boat at the starting line. The men had removed their jackets and rolled up their sleeves, preparing to heave sails into place. Camberly was barking orders and Alasdair called a laughing response back to him.

The scene through her binoculars warmed Marianne's heart. This time she'd found real friends and this circle of wonderful friends would continue to stand by her as she adjusted to life in England. Since their engagement had become official, Marianne had started to realize all it would mean to stay in England. San Francisco was a long way away. Her parents would return home, but she would not. She had not recognized that as a possible consequence when she'd set out on her journey. When she'd left the beautiful mansion in San Francisco, the only home in which she'd ever lived, she'd never imagined that she wouldn't be coming back. But neither could she now imagine being without Alasdair. He was her world now.

Marianne lowered the binoculars, taking a moment

to ingest the depth of her realizations: a new world, new friends. On either side of her sat two women who'd made the same choices she had.

On her right sat Audrey St. Clair-Maddox, who'd left her home in New York and risked her career as a pianist to become Camberly's wife. On her left, Stella Carrington had risked everything in the opposite direction. She'd been born the daughter of an earl, destined from an early age to make an important marriage to another great house. Instead, she had given up her right to a title when she'd married Lionel, a rich American without one. There were those who thought she'd chosen poorly. But one could not doubt the rightness of her choice when one saw the obvious affection she and Lionel felt for one another. Those that supported Stella's marriage were quick to remind the opposition that a daughter of an earl would always be a daughter of an earl no matter whom she married, and that their children would be the grandchildren of an earl regardless of their father's antecedents.

Marianne knew it would not be easy for her as Alasdair's countess. But the presence of Stella and Audrey reminded her that it could be done and that it was worth being done.

A starting gun went off and the boats on the line leapt to life, sails jerking to catch the wind. This would be the first of many races. The regatta lasted nearly a week and all types of boats would race by class.

Marianne put her binoculars to her eyes again to

catch a last glimpse of Alasdair before the boat was lost to sight. The race was a long one and she didn't expect to see the boat again until after lunch. Some of the yachts had posted themselves out farther in the water to trail the sailboats, but her group had opted to save that for another day. Today there was a market set up in town to take advantage of the presence of so many noble guests. They were going shopping. Marianne was looking forward to strolling the colorful booths with Audrey and Stella. Her parents and Lionel were staying behind.

Once the boats were lost to sight, the three women gathered up their parasols and reticules. The market was set up near the piers to catch the most foot traffic. The women admired the booths, pausing to buy a few small trinkets and souvenirs that commemorated the event. Marianne bought a program that resembled a playbill, listing all the boats, the races, and the dates of sailing.

Stella stopped at one booth to look at some French-milled soap. The crowd was especially thick here, and Audrey and Marianne stood back a little way from the booth to avoid the brunt of it. That was when it happened.

A knot of men crashed through the crowd quite suddenly, reeling as if drunk. Marianne saw Audrey step out of the way, but one of them ran into her anyway, causing her to stagger backward. Audrey might have fallen if a passing gentleman hadn't stopped to catch her. Marianne had been about to dart forward, toward her friend, when she felt something hard jab into her side.

That was when she realized that the reeling group of men now effectively obscured Audrey from her sight. If she couldn't see Audrey, then Audrey couldn't see her.

"Come with me, Miss Addison, so that no harm is done," a low voice spoke roughly in her ear.

She twisted to look at the man but she did not recognize him. "No, you don't know me. The boss wouldn't be that stupid, miss." The man jabbed the hard object into her ribs again. "Come along."

Marianne drew a deep steadying breath. The hard object felt like the barrel of a small gun. She knew a moment's panic as her mind tried to focus on the improbable: she was being marched out of the market, in plain sight of hundreds, by a man with a covert gun. She was being kidnapped and no one suspected a thing.

Her mind quickly ran over her options. Should she try his mettle and scream? Would he really shoot her, especially since he'd made it clear that he worked for someone else? Probably he wouldn't shoot her, but she did worry that he might not hesitate to shoot someone else who attempted to come to her aid.

Her captor roughly pushed her along the emptier side streets. Marianne focused on remembering directions as they twisted away from the narrow High Street that defined the main part of town.

"You can look all you like, miss," the man said gruffly. "The boss won't be keeping you here long enough for it to matter."

Marianne's spirits sank. That explained why there hadn't been an attempt to blindfold her once they'd cleared the crowd. The good news was that at least no one was planning on killing her, just moving her. She should be thankful.

They reached a doorway in a decrepit-looking building and he shoved her inside. The interior stank of mildew, mold, and other smells Marianne didn't care to put a name to. Perhaps it was better for those scents to go unrecognized.

"Come in, my dear." A man stood at the shuttered window where the only pieces of furniture in the room were placed: a rickety table and two equally rickety chairs.

The voice sounded vaguely familiar. Marianne let her eyes adjust to the dim room. "Have a seat, Miss Addison. The chair's clean even if it looks a bit unstable. I promise it won't collapse."

Marianne stepped near the table simply to get a closer look at the man. A frisson of fear shot through her as she recognized his features. Lord Brantley. He had never seemed particularly wholesome to her even in the best of lights the few times she'd seen him, but today in the grim interior of this room, he appeared positively evil. A sneer marked his face as he swept her a mockingly gallant bow, his eyes cold with calculation.

"No one saw you, I trust?" he asked his henchman.

The man gave a malevolent grin. "No, it worked just like you said, boss."

"Very good. That means we have plenty of time to discuss your situation, Miss Addison."

Marianne said nothing as he sat down across from her, spearing her with a gaze that made her skin crawl, his intentions obvious and revolting.

"I hear congratulations are in order on your forthcoming nuptials. I am glad to say that those will proceed, but perhaps your groom will be . . . a bit changed. Of course, that's all up to you.

"I have a boat waiting for us in a quiet cove where we won't be detected by the racers. That boat will convey us to Ryde, a small village down the coast where we can be married later today. I have a special license of course."

Marianne met his gaze steadily, steeling herself not to flinch at his proposition. "Why would I marry you when I have a perfectly good groom of my own picked out?"

"I am assuming you would prefer Pennington to live, or have I misjudged your affections?" Brantley inquired with an air of feigned innocence. "It's very simple, my dear. I have men waiting for Pennington when he returns to port. They have been instructed to either see to his demise or to deliver the message that you have chosen another. Which will it be?"

"You know very well that you've offered me no

choice at all," Marianne returned coldly. All she could buy herself and Alasdair was time. She had no misguided naïveté causing her to believe that her decision would avert the potential for bloodshed. Brantley was mad with revenge; she could see it in the intensity of his cold eyes. Her choice could merely prevent Alasdair from being taken unawares. At least now, he would be prepared and forewarned about the intentions of his foe. But a fight was coming—it was inevitable.

Alasdair jumped down to the pier and threw the last mooring rope, firmly anchoring their schooner to the dock. Camberly clambered down behind him, slapping him on the back. "Good sailing today."

"Second isn't too bad. At least the Kaiser finished third. That'll keep Bertie happy for another year," Alasdair joked. "Those American boats are getting faster every year. The boat that beat us picked up the wind like nothing I've ever seen."

They walked to the Addison boat in good humor, talking over the day's race. Alasdair put a sudden hand on Camberly's arms. "Wait, something seems odd." They both stopped and studied the deck of the yacht.

"They should be outside, watching for us. The boat appears empty." A quick lurch of fear spurred Alasdair on. Marianne should be waving a flag—she should have been on deck cheering him on as he came into port. He took the steps two at a time, Camberly close behind.

They found the group gathered inside the cabin. Audrey rose and came to them immediately, her face chalky. "Marianne is gone. I fear it's a kidnapping. She disappeared in the marketplace."

Alasdair sat down hard in the closest chair. "Brantley is behind this." He regretted his choice of means to expose Brantley's blackmail. Instead of thwarting Brantley and destroying the rest of his ammunition, Alasdair felt he'd merely provided tinder to start a bigger fire. Now Marianne was at physical risk. She was somewhere alone with the bastard right now. He hoped she had the good sense to be scared instead of being bold and forthright. Brantley would not stand for that and it would make her lot worse.

Audrey related the events in the market, recounting the rowdy men that had separated them in the street. It definitely sounded planned. The act itself wasn't all that complicated, but timing made all the difference. Brantley hadn't needed an intricate plot because he'd known that Alasdair would be out to sea all day. Alasdair had no idea where to track them. Was Brantley hiding out in the city somewhere, waiting for the crowds to die down before he risked leaving Cowes with her? Had he slipped out of town already? If so, it would have had to be by boat. The Isle of Wight was a literal island. If by boat, which way had they gone? Had he headed back to England or had he headed through the Channel for France? Worse, perhaps he'd gone by land, deeper into the countryside of the isle?

Alasdair and the others talked through the grim options. He wanted to discard the last notion, that Brantley had taken her inland, but Camberly was hesitant. "Before we can discard any alternatives, we need to think about what Brantley's goals are."

"He wants to win that blasted wager at White's by disgracing her, but even more than that, he wants to get back at me for stealing what he felt was his heiress," Alasdair said dully.

A knock sounded on the cabin door. One of the deckhands entered. "An invitation has arrived." He passed a salver to Camberly, who was closest to the door.

"An invitation? How odd," Stella said curiously.

Camberly opened it and passed it Alasdair. "Not so odd, considering the circumstances."

Alasdair grimaced. "It seems we are invited to a wedding in Ryde. We have our answer. He means to marry her."

"He's even given us a time for the ceremony," Camberly pointed out. "He means to marry her and he means for you to see him do it."

Alasdair swallowed hard. The implication of the invitation wasn't lost on him. "Get a map. How far is Ryde?"

Lionel produced a map and spread it on the table. Alasdair made a quick calculation. "It will be quicker to sail down the coast than to go overland."

"The winds are coming up—we noticed it the last leg of the race," Camberly cautioned.

Alasdair shook his head. "I know, but we'll never get there in time by land and it would mean having to find horses to rent in a crowded town. It's got to be the boat."

Even with the wind picking up, the Addisons' steamer would make good time, he told himself. The Addison boat had all the latest advancements available. This boat was their best chance to rescue Marianne. The alternative was unfathomable.

"Do you think the guests will make it?" Brantley asked under the veneer of polite conversation. He flipped open his pocket watch. "Twenty minutes to go, my dear." They sat in the front pews of a rustic church in the village of Ryde, having made the journey that afternoon in a boat.

Marianne said nothing. She continued to stare straight ahead and maintain her silence. Alasdair would come, but then what? He couldn't very well bring any authorities with him. This was a private quarrel and it would be dealt with in a private manner. But would Alasdair come in time? Brantley had constantly reminded her that, guests or not, the wedding would take place. He'd even forced her to put on a frothy confection of a wedding dress he'd had on board the rented craft. The dress was cheap and clearly secondhand. Marianne could detect the smell of the previous owner's stale perfume. Neither she nor Brantley smelled particularly fresh in their wedding attire. He reeked of old cigar smoke and Marianne missed the clean scent of Alasdair's herbs and lavender.

The only time she'd spoken since their arrival in Ryde had been to protest her unwillingness to the vicar, who hadn't taken her pleas seriously against the money Brantley had pressed in his palm.

"It will be better this way, my dear," Brantley said. "You know next to nothing about being a countess. You'd never have been good enough—his mother would have seen to that." He let out an exaggerated breath. "You're actually lucky to escape that harridan for a mother-in-law. My parents are both deceased, so there's no one to bother you. You'll find that I am easy to live with as long as I have money."

He snapped open the watch again and Marianne fought the urge to look at the back door of the chapel. She would not let him see how unnerved she was becoming. "Five minutes. Close enough. I guess it will just be the two of us." He stood up and smoothed his trousers. "Perhaps he didn't love you as much as you thought. It's better to find out this way instead of after marrying him. At least with me, there are no illusions, no pretenses."

The vicar took his place at the front of the church. "You have witnesses?"

"Yes," Brantley said confidently. "I have my man there." He gestured to the man who'd removed Marianne from the marketplace, his gun still lodged inside his jacket where it had remained all afternoon as a form of subtle encouragement. Two others who had crewed the boat sat facing the back door, on alert in case the "guests" arrived.

Marianne rose and tried again: "Vicar, I do not wish to marry him."

"Silence," Brantley barked at her, his grip on her arm hurtful.

Marianne was bolder this time. "You can't shoot me—there's no money in it. There's no one else to shoot here that I care about," she railed. "Are you going to have your men shoot one another? They've been awful to me so go ahead—I won't stop you. When Alasdair arrives there won't be anyone for you to hide behind." She knew a moment's victory. There was nothing he could say to that.

"Start the ceremony, Vicar," Brantley growled, one of his henchmen waving a gun when the vicar would have wavered, upon finally having discovered his conscience. While Marianne didn't have a care over who was shot, he certainly did, especially when it came to his own head. The gun held plenty of influence for him.

Brantley yanked Marianne up to the altar steps, and whatever surreal quality the afternoon possessed evaporated. Fear came to her for the first time. She was going to end up married to Brantley. Alasdair wasn't going to arrive in time.

"The short version please," Brantley demanded, but

she heard him only dimly because he was in the periphery of her thoughts. Her other thoughts were on Alasdair. At least he was alive. She'd done this to keep him from being shot down on the pier. She had no doubts that Brantley would have seen it done.

Soon it would be too late. The vicar had arrived at the moment when they exchanged their own pledges. Marianne refused. "I won't do it. I won't say the words."

Brantley scoffed. "You might as well say them. You're ruined already if it hasn't escaped your attention. You've been alone with a man, a man with whom you've eloped. You will not be able to go back and reclaim your reputation after you've been with me. There would always be doubt." It was the meanest thing he'd said to her all afternoon. From telling her how unsuitable she was to be a countess, to how likely it was that she would fail miserably to please Alasdair, this was the meanest by far.

"Perhaps he knows it already and that is why he hasn't come," Brantley hissed. "I can always have him shot. It doesn't have to be today. But you can save him, dear. He will be my wedding gift to you."

"I can think of a better wedding gift." A familiar voice came from the back of the church. Marianne knew an achingly sweet relief. She turned to see Alasdair, and Camberly, and Lionel, and a few men she didn't know crowding the small church, weapons pointed at the two men who had been acting as guards.

Alasdair advanced on Brantley, anger emanating from every pore. Marianne made a surreptitious move away from Brantley, but she wasn't fast enough. He grabbed for her and pulled her close, finding a small gun of his own in his coat pocket.

"Stay where you are, Pennington. She's my hostage, my surety for my freedom. She comes with me. I'll release her when I am in France."

"No," Alasdair answered evenly. "Your surety is that she is released to me and you may get on your boat and sail to France never to return. I have it on good authority from the prince himself that those are the best odds you'll see for some time. You're not welcome in England anymore."

Marianne could feel Brantley weighing the options available to him. She could feel his resignation, the tenseness of his body easing as he let her go, giving her a vicious thrust toward Alasdair.

A cry erupted from the back. "Get down! He's going to shoot!" It was Lionel. Marianne reacted immediately, feeling Alasdair on top of her, covering her protectively with his large form. A gun fired, sounding more like a cannon from somewhere in the tiny church. Marianne heard herself scream. Alasdair pressed down on her more firmly, giving her his strength.

"It's all right," Lionel called out, waving his long rifle. "I've only clipped him."

Marianne felt Alasdair lift himself off her. "Are you all right?" He helped her gain her feet.

She was shaking now, realizing how close it had all come to being over. "I think so." But she took the opportunity to sink back into Alasdair's strong embrace.

Lionel strode with Camberly to the front of the church where Brantley clutched his shoulder. "We'll see to him and get him escorted to the boat. The others will disperse the rabble." Lionel jerked his Winchester at the hired men.

Marianne let Alasdair guide her from the church. "You came," Marianne said simply.

"Of course I did. Did you think I wouldn't?" Alasdair held her close not caring about propriety. "I was worried sick that the boat wouldn't be fast enough. I was worried you'd been harmed. You are all right, aren't you?"

"I am fine." They'd originally decided on a December wedding in the country, to appease his mother, but suddenly December seemed too far away. "Do you know what I am thinking?" she asked quietly. "I'm thinking I don't want to wait for Christmas. I want to be married when we get back to London or Devonshire, or wherever it is that we're going next."

"I'm thinking you're right." Alasdair grinned in the dusky twilight.

Marianne drew back, shaky. Her hands swiped at the tears dampening her face. Alasdair chuckled and offered her a handkerchief. "There's no reason to cry, Marianne. Hasn't anyone ever told you there's no use crying over spilled champagne?"

Marianne laughed through her tears. "I thought it was milk."

"Not in this case." He bent to catch her lips again, this time in a kiss that wiped away any thought of tears and promised only the very best of happily-ever-afters.

Epilogue

Three years later

"Mmmm, what smells so good?" Alasdair poked his head into the kitchen at Highborough, a room that had always been large in order to accommodate the amount of space needed to prepare food in massive quantities, but which had grown even grander the past three years with the addition of an enormous bread oven imported from San Francisco, along with several other modern culinary conveniences.

"We're making bread, Daddy!" his two-year-old son, William, said as he looked up from his stool where he sat next to Marianne at the long worktable. She was instructing him in the art of bread making.

Alasdair strode across the room to join them. "It looks like you're doing a good job," he said, although

Alasdair privately thought that William was more interested in making a dusty mess with the flour than he was in making a neat loaf of bread.

Marianne caught his eye. "Did you know, William, that when I first met your dad, he couldn't make a bed or make bread?"

"Really?" William asked in amazement.

Marianne smiled softly across the table at Alasdair, her hand going to the gentle mound just starting to show beneath her apron. There would be another child in a few months, another child for his dream of having a real family. It was her dream, too, and he loved her all the more for it.

Each day Highborough became a place he loved more and more. He loved seeing William's toys in the drawing room. He loved having to kick a ball out of his path as he made his way to his study. He loved having William play in his study as he did estate business while Marianne read a book just a few feet away. It was true that Highborough had benefited from his wife's dowry, but not all of her dowry was financial. Alasdair could not begin to calculate the ways she'd changed his life—ways that went for beyond the value of a dollar. She'd changed the lives of those around them too.

Sarah Stewart, upon Marianne's encouragement, moved into the dower house on their property and began traveling. Alasdair's mother saw her dream of joining the Stewart and Pennington properties by marrying

Sarah's father herself, and moving into his estate, leaving Marianne and Alasdair alone at Highborough.

If Highborough had a few more nicks in the wood and a few more scratches on the floor, it was easily offset by the weekly smell of bread baking in the kitchens and the purple of Romagna blooming in the flower beds.

Alasdair reached across the table and wiped a smear of flour from Marianne's cheek, and she smiled at him, her love for him obvious in her eyes. He was the luckiest of men and he knew it. Love had found him in the form of his sourdough heiress, an unlikely madcap from San Francisco. Alasdair smiled back at Marianne. Love had found him when he'd least expected it. Indeed, he'd never seen it coming.